SECOND CHANCES AT THE STABLES ON MUDDYPUDDLE LANE

Heart-warming, uplifting romance

Etti Summers

CHAPTER ONE

Beth peered through her nets and frowned in annoyance. Anita, her next-door neighbour, had put her bins out again. That in itself wasn't an issue. Where she had put them **was**. Why couldn't the bloody woman put them outside her own gate?

Why did she have to butt them up against Beth's? It made it look like Beth had double the number of bins to anyone else in the street. That blimmin' dog of Anita's had also woken her up in the early hours, barking its head off. And don't get her started on the kids. The woman was forever shouting at them, screeching at the top of her voice, day in, day out. And the little sods didn't take a blind bit of notice, so Anita might as well save her breath and save Beth from having to listen to it.

Tightening the belt of her dressing gown, Beth stomped into the hall, yanked open the front door and marched down the short path. Muttering under her breath, she dragged her neighbour's bins back to where they belonged – in front of her neighbour's house. And for good measure, she deposited them right in front of the gate. If the woman wanted to get out, she'd have to shift them.

Beth knew she was being petty, but since she'd retired a few months ago, she didn't have much else to think about, and the issues with the woman next door were gradually taking on bigger and bigger proportions.

'Oi! What do you think you're doing?' Anita yelled through her bedroom window.

Beth smiled sweetly. 'Just putting these back where they belong.'

'They're blocking my gate. Damien will be wanting to go to school in a minute.'

From the amount of yelling the bloody woman had done just to get Damien out of bed, Beth was pretty certain the boy didn't want to go to school at all.

'So, move them,' Beth called back, and turned on her slippered heel to march up the pavement and back inside.

Slamming the door with more force than was strictly necessary, she went into the kitchen to make herself a cup of tea, and whilst the kettle came to the boil, she thought about what she would do today.

The oven could do with a good clean and there was a bit of washing in the laundry basket, but probably not enough for a full load. There was a time when the washing machine was always on the go, but that had been when the kids were little. They were all grown up now, with washing machines of their own. Except for Maisie. There wasn't room for a washing machine in the static that she lived in with her boyfriend Adam, so when she wanted to do any washing, she borrowed Dulcie's.

The kettle's automatic switch knocked off, and Beth wondered why the hell she was thinking about washing machines... Oh yes, half a load. She would wait until the end of the week and see what was in the laundry basket then. If she still didn't have enough for a full load, she would chuck in a few tea towels. They could always do with a freshen-up.

Beth made a cup of tea, mashing the tea bag against the side of the mug with a spoon.

She could pop to the supermarket later. She had a few bits to get, and it meant she would have some fresh air – although how fresh it was, being in the city, was debatable.

Dulcie had fresh air. Loads of it. Well, she would, wouldn't she, being halfway up a hillside in the middle of nowhere. Those goats she kept didn't smell too good though, and the chicken coop reeked.

What was she doing now, Beth wondered. There was one way to find out: she would call her. But after listening to twelve rings, Beth gave up. Her middle daughter was probably outside doing farming stuff.

How about Nikki? But when Beth checked the time, she realised that her eldest child would probably be on her way to work. Jay didn't pick up either, and although Maisie answered after the third ring (one day that girl would have to have her phone surgically removed), she sounded out of breath.

'Am I allowed to ask why you sound like you've just run a marathon?' Beth asked.

'We're moving stones.'

Of course she was. What else did one do on a Thursday morning?

Maisie was obviously busy, so Beth said, 'I'll let you get on, but be careful you don't put your back out. It can ruin the rest of your life, can a bad back.'

'I'll be fine, Mum. Stop fussing.'

Beth hung up, muttering, 'That's what mothers do – fuss.' Not that any of her kids appreciated or cared just how much she worried about them. That was the privilege and arrogance of youth: they thought they were invincible. And the younger they were, the more invincible they thought they were.

Nikki, being the eldest, was starting to have an inkling that life was harsher and less forgiving than she'd assumed, but she wasn't there yet. She would soon change her tune when she was staring middle age in the face and wondering where the grey hair, wrinkles, and saggy boobs had come from.

Where had all the years gone? One minute Beth had been dancing in the Plaz, flares flapping around her legs, a disco ball pixelating her skin and the taste of Snake

Bite on her tongue; and the next, she was rubbing her bunions and wondering where she could buy support stockings. The bit in between was a blur of nappies, nits and teenage strops. In those days she had longed for an hour to herself, a bit of peace and quiet where nobody was demanding anything of her.

'Be careful what you wish for,' she grumbled, startled when she realised she'd said it out loud. Flipping heck, she was talking to herself now. Maybe she should get a cat? There was a distinct similarity between cats and daughters: they were both disdainful (scornful, even), they both treated their homes like a hotel, and they both came and went as they pleased at all hours of the day and night, but at least cats didn't answer back.

Beth sighed disconsolately. She would give her right arm to have one of her kids answer her back right now. The house was too big and too silent, except for the echoes as she rattled around in it.

Should she find something smaller? It would certainly be less to clean. Not that there was much cleaning to be done now that her youngest had moved out.

Was it because of **her** that all of them had moved away? Had she been such a bad mother that at the first opportunity to leave Birmingham (and her) they'd leapt at it?

She tried to console herself with the thought that at least her daughters were still in the country, unlike Jay who couldn't have gone any further away if he'd tried.

As long as they were happy, that was all that mattered she told herself, ignoring the inner voice that wanted to know whether **she** was happy. And if she wasn't, didn't she deserve to be?

But how could she be happy when she was so damned lonely?

 Annoyed at having such negative thoughts, Beth tried to count her blessings. And she was the first to admit that she had many: she was healthy, her kids were healthy, she had a nice little pension to top up her OAP pension, she had a roof over her head... It should be enough, but it wasn't. Beth missed her kids, and there was nothing she could do about it. **Or was there?**

Walter removed his brown corduroy trousers from the back of the chair in his bedroom, stared at them, then put them back. Even he had to admit that they had seen better days. He was going for tea at the farm, not mucking out a sheep shed, so he had better wear something halfway decent, or Otto would be giving him concerned looks out of the corner of his eye.

The same went for the checked flannel shirt and the khaki-green pullover that he liked to wear over the top.

Walter opened his wardrobe door. Now, where was the nice shirt that Nikki and Gio had given him for Christmas? Ah, there it was, hanging next to his funeral suit.

Slipping the shirt off the hanger, he put it on, stiff fingers struggling with the buttons. He had a bit of arthritis in his hands, and sometimes it played him up.

A tidy pair of trousers later, and he decided he scrubbed up okay. His hair was getting a bit long though, so when he went downstairs he put a note on the calendar as a reminder to make an appointment with the barber.

Having supper at the farmhouse was a rare treat these days. Poor Otto was usually so busy, what with running the restaurant, training new chefs for Alistair (his old boss when he used to live in London), and working on another foraging cookbook, that Walter hardly saw him.

He wished his son didn't work so hard, but Otto had a passion which couldn't be denied. And Dulcie was no better. The girl was holding down a day job as well as running the farm and starting a new business.

Walter reflected sadly that it didn't used to be like that in his day. Farmers were farmers back then; they didn't usually have to go get a second job to make ends meet. He blamed the government. And the supermarket chains for being too greedy. So many farmers today were packing it in, that very soon there wouldn't be any farms left.

Walter continued to fret about the state of British farming all the way up the lane. He didn't envy youngsters today – they always seemed so busy. Mind you, he hadn't sat on his backside twiddling his thumbs. He had worked damned hard. He'd had to. Farming wasn't a nine-to-five, Monday-to-Friday job, with weekends off.

He had bloody loved it though, despite it almost being the death of him. Walter still couldn't bear to think about how he had managed to run up so much debt and how ill he had become as a result, without feeling ashamed. Having to get rid of the farm had been one of the darkest times of his life, but he recognised that it had to be done. It didn't stop him from missing the old place though, and he tried to help out when and where he could. The problem was that Otto continued to fret and fuss if he thought Walter was doing too much. And whilst it was lovely that his son cared about his welfare, Walter was bored rigid.

Now that he felt better in himself (and he had done for a good long while), he missed being busy. And although he hated to admit it, he was lonely. Even Amos at the stables, who was roughly the same age as him (give or take a few years) didn't have enough hours in the day. What with helping out with the holiday lets, looking after his great-nephew, baby Amory, and having found love with Lena, Amos was constantly on the go. Whereas Walter always seemed to be searching around for something to do.

As usual, Walter had Peg with him, and the dog darted ahead into the farmhouse, announcing his arrival. A wall of delicious cooking smells hit him when he stepped inside.

'Hi, Dad.' Otto was at the stove, stirring and tossing, several pans and pots on the go.

Dulcie was in the dining room, laying the table. Walter had never used that room for dining in, preferring to eat his meals at the kitchen table. It was these little changes, probably more than the big ones (such as the farm no longer having a flock of sheep), that made him realise every time he visited that this was no longer his home.

Brushing his sadness aside, he hurried towards Dulcie to give her a kiss. 'Do you need a hand with anything?' he asked, after he had greeted her.

'No thanks, Walter, it's all under control.' Dulcie always said that, even though he could tell that it sometimes wasn't, and he knew the reason was that she and Otto worried he might become ill again if he overdid it.

Fat chance of that! He was more likely to die of boredom these days.

'How is the soap-making coming along?' he asked, over dinner.

Dulcie had recently invested in a small herd of goats and was using their milk to make soap and other lotions and potions, and Otto also made the most wonderful ice cream with it.

'Slow but steady,' she replied, around a mouthful of aromatic beef. 'I've been experimenting with new scents and adding different flowers into the mix.'

Walter had been given a few samples to try in the past, and he must admit that the soaps did smell nice. Dulcie packaged them beautifully, too. Her soap was a quality product.

'Lavender, rose and vanilla are still my best sellers though,' she added. 'I'm thinking of planting some lavender bushes in the orchard, but I'm not sure whether they'll like it there.'

'If you want a hand, give me a shout,' he offered.

'Thanks Walter, but I've got it covered. Maisie likes planting things.'

'How is she getting on at the old farmhouse?' he asked.

Never in a million years did he think that the derelict farmhouse on the mountain above, could be brought back to life. He'd assumed it was too far gone, but from what Dulcie was saying, Maisie and her fella were making a go of it.

'It's going to take time,' Dulcie said, 'because they're concentrating on getting the business side of things up and running first.'

'Have they decided what they're going to do with it?'

'Kennels, I believe. But don't take my word for it – Maisie changes her mind like the wind.'

Walter thought he might go take a look. It was a long time since he had ventured onto the hillside above the farm, and he wondered if they'd managed to improve the track that led onto the mountain. A few weeks back, he had watched with interest as a lorry had hauled an ancient static caravan up Muddypuddle Lane, wincing as it had inched its way up the narrow road.

He hoped the caravan was well insulated because the top of the mountain could be a windswept place, and he didn't envy Maisie and her fella living in it come winter. Still, youngsters didn't feel the cold like old folk did, and Walter couldn't deny that he was old. His aching joints were eager to remind him every morning. But again, that could be due to sitting on his behind for most of the day. Use it or lose it, wasn't that how the saying went?

The way Walter was going, he would seize up before long, so maybe a nice walk to the top of the mountain would do him good, and he could pop in and see Maisie and her caravan at the same time.

Beth parked her little red car in one of Picklewick's side streets, and tried to pretend that she wasn't being furtive. Telling herself that she had every right to be in the village (she did) and that she wasn't obliged to tell her children that she was here (she wasn't), Beth nevertheless scurried along the high street.

When she came to the building she was aiming for, she glanced up and down the road before darting inside.

She was scanning the properties in the 'To Rent' section (there were only a handful) and looking for the one she wanted, when she sensed someone approaching.

'Those are our rental properties,' a young chap said. By 'young' Beth meant that he was in his late twenties.

'I realise that,' she replied.

'Is it a rental property you're after?'

Why would she be looking at rental properties if she wasn't thinking about renting one? She didn't mean to send him a withering look, but his slight recoil made her aware that she must have.

'Is it for yourself?' he battled on.

'Why wouldn't it be?'

'It's just a standard question, madam.'

She pressed her lips together before replying. 'Yes, it's for me.'

'How many beds are you after?'

Beth lost patience. 'Let's cut to the chase. You've got a two up, two down terraced on your website. I would like to take a look at it, please.'

'Hazelnut Road? It has just become available.'

'Can I take a look?' Beth repeated.

'Let me check the diary.'

'I want to see it today. Right now, preferably.'

'I'm not sure that will be possible. We operate an appointment system for viewings and—'

'I've driven all the way from Birmingham this morning, for the sole purpose of taking a look at it.'

'I'm sorry; if you had phoned, we would—'

'I did. I was told I could see it today.'

'Ah, right.' The young man was studying his computer screen. 'Who did you speak to?'

'No idea.'

'There's nothing in the diary.'

'Is everything okay, Zander?' An older gentleman had stepped out of an office and was gazing at Beth with curiosity.

'This lady says she has an appointment to view the new instruction on Hazelnut Road, but there isn't anything in the diary.'

'It's vacant, isn't it?'

'I believe so.'

'In that case, can you hold the fort for half an hour, whilst I take this client to view it?'

Beth breathed a sigh of relief. The organ grinder had come to her rescue, leaving the poor monkey still searching the electronic diary for a non-existent appointment.

Beth felt a smidgen of remorse for fibbing to the young lad, but not enough to come clean. Even if she hadn't been able to wrangle a viewing, she would have peeped in through the windows. It had looked nice in the photographs, so she was quietly hopeful it would be just as nice in real life.

Ten minutes later saw the estate agent unlocking the front door and gesturing for her to step inside.

It wasn't big, but it would do. The front door opened directly into the living room, which probably had enough space for a three-piece suite and a table to eat at. At the rear was the kitchen, leading to a small back garden with a little yard. Upstairs were two good-sized bedrooms and a bathroom. The only thing she wasn't too keen on, was that the stairs were in the lounge. However, it wasn't a deal breaker.

The house had been freshly painted, and was clean and empty of furniture.

'I'll take it,' she announced. 'When can I move in? Monday?'

'It's not that simple, Mrs Fairfax. We have to obtain references, and we'll need to draw up a rental agreement, then there's the deposit to discuss.'

'Well?' she demanded. 'What are you waiting for? Let's get the ball rolling.'

The sooner she moved in, the sooner she would be in the heart of her family again. Her idea to move to Picklewick was a genius one! Wait until she told her girls: they would be thrilled.

But she wouldn't tell them just yet. She would tell them when everything was signed and sealed. It would be a lovely surprise.

Walter paused to catch his breath for what felt like the hundredth time, Peg panting by his side. She seemed equally as glad of the momentary rest, but then again, she had covered more ground than him, having dashed around from the second they'd set off.

Surely the hill never used to be this steep? Grudgingly, he supposed that the climb would seem harder – after all, the last time he had been up this way on foot would have been several years ago, and when he had been in better health. The further up the mountain he went, the more frequently he stopped to take in the view. That was his excuse, and he intended to stick with it.

Determined not to let the incline beat him, Walter pushed on, his tread slow and ponderous. By the time the old farmhouse came into view, his breathing was laboured and his legs were in agony, but he felt a spark of pride that he'd done it.

Eighteen months ago his son had been so worried about him that he had quit his marvellous job in London to come home to look after him. And look at him now – able to walk to the top of the mountain and onto the common, completely under his own steam.

But whether he would be able to get out of his chair tomorrow without help, was a different matter entirely.

Now that the gradient had lost its bite, Walter was able to pick up the pace a bit as he made his way to Maisie and Adam's new place. Technically it belonged to Adam, because it was he who had bought it from Dulcie, but Maisie was his girlfriend (or partner, as she referred to herself) and she lived there too. Not in the farmhouse, because that was just as derelict as the last time he had clapped eyes on it, but in the caravan that he'd watched being hauled up the lane.

It was a miracle they'd managed to get it onto the mountain, but there it was, perched on breeze blocks to keep it off the ground.

He could see two figures labouring over a pile of stones, moving them from one place to another, and a wave of nostalgia swept through him. When he was a boy, this used to be a working farm. He distinctly remembered the elderly couple who used to own it. But the old chap had died, and his wife had followed shortly after, and none of their kids had wanted to take it on. Grown up and with no room for a hill farm in their lives, they had been happy to sell it to Walter's dad for a song.

The outbuildings had been in a bad state of repair even then, but they'd been okay for storing winter feed. Nowadays there was little left of them, aside from a pile of hand-chiselled stone and the footprint of where they used to be.

'Walter!' Maisie had spotted him and came hurrying over. 'What are you doing here? Does Otto know?'

'Why should he? He's my son, not my keeper,' he snapped, then was instantly remorseful. Maisie was only looking out for him. 'I came to see what all the fuss is about,' he said, more kindly. 'I see you're making progress.'

'Slowly,' Maisie said, leading him towards Adam, who was watching him approach.

'Have you come to lend a hand?' Adam asked, shaking hands with him.

'Not on your nelly. That looks like hard work!'

'It is.'

'That's good stone, that is. Are you going to reuse it?'

'You bet we are. But not here. We're going to use it to repair the house and build an extension.'

Walter admired the young man's vision as he talked him through their plans.

'The biggest problem is getting materials on site. The track from Dulcie's farm onto the mountain needs to be tarmacked, and that's going to cost a fortune.' Adam looked so down in the mouth, that Walter's heart went out to him.

He scratched his whiskery chin. 'I've got an idea. There's a forestry track that runs up through the trees over that way.' He pointed to a dark green patch of conifers that had been planted decades ago and had now grown to maturity.

The trees flanked the sides of a hill a fair distance from the old farmhouse, but the logging road running through them was hard-packed gravel and wasn't nearly as steep as the track above Dulcie's farm.

As Walter described it to him, Adam's expression brightened. 'I'll take a look right now,' he said. 'Do you want to come with me?'

'No thanks, lad. I'm knackered. I'll have a quick cuppa with Maisie while she tells me what she's going to do with those sheds once they're built, then I'm off home.'

'I can give you a lift, if you like?'

Walter shook his head. 'You get on and check out that old logging road. I got up here by myself – I'll make it down by myself.'

He had a feeling he would regret not taking Adam up on his offer, but he was nothing if not stubborn. And he probably had more pride than was good for him. But, darn it, he hated being thought of as old and incapable, and he wanted to make himself useful.

Hopefully, he had done that today, and if that was the case having stiff joints and aching muscles tomorrow would be a small price to pay.

CHAPTER TWO

Beth peered through her nets and frowned in annoyance. Anita, her next-door neighbour, had put her bins out again. That in itself wasn't an issue. Where she had put them **was**. Why couldn't the bloody woman put them outside her own gate?

'That's all of it,' Amir announced, holding onto the attic ladder with one hand and balancing a cardboard box on his shoulder with the other. He set it down carefully on the landing, alongside the others, and dusted his hands off.

'Can I make you a cup of tea?' Beth asked hopefully. Anything to delay having to sort them out.

'I'm alright thanks, Mrs Fairfax. I'd better get on. I've got lectures this afternoon.'

Beth tried to press a twenty-pound note into his palm 'for his trouble,' but he refused that as well, so she waved him off, thankful that her neighbour was so kind. She never would have managed to get up the attic on her own.

It was a long time since she'd seen what was up there, but from what she remembered much of it was junk.

As she opened the flap of the nearest box, she couldn't for the life of her work out why she had hung onto an old iron that didn't work, or that vase, considering she had never liked it. Beth anticipated that she would be making several trips to the household waste recycling centre, and she was quite looking forward to it, as she'd never been there before. Not surprising, since she'd only recently bought a car.

She chuckled as she remembered the look on Dulcie and Maisie's faces when she'd rocked up at the farm in it at Easter. Dulcie had feared that she was going to insist on staying longer than the fortnight she'd planned, but her middle daughter needn't have worried; Beth hadn't had any intention of staying. And she had no intention of staying now, not when she would have a home of her own in Picklewick.

A twinge of conscience pricked her: she hadn't told her children what she'd done. She would have to at some point, but not yet, not until it was irreversible. Actually, it was irreversible now, since she had given notice on this place and had taken out a lease on her new one. There was no going back. But she was nevertheless reluctant to tell her kids. Jay, in New Zealand, probably wouldn't mind, but the girls were a different matter.

She honestly didn't know what their reaction would be. She hoped they would understand that she missed them. All three now lived in Picklewick, so was it so wrong for her to want to be near them?

As she settled into her task of sorting out more than three decades of living in this house, Beth prayed they wouldn't be too upset. She knew how irritated they could get with her, and she didn't mean to be annoying, but no matter what she did or said, one or the other of them would get cross.

At times she felt like she was the child and Nikki or Dulcie was the parent. Not so much with Maisie, because her youngest still acted more like a teenager than an adult. Although, to be fair, since Maisie had met Adam, she was less fifteen and more twenty-five, which was her actual age.

Aw, look, Nikki's first pair of proper shoes!

A wave of sadness enveloped Beth, both for the time long gone and for her firstborn who was now a mother herself. And a smidgen of guilt followed quickly in its wake as she realised that she hadn't kept any of her other children's first pairs of shoes. And neither had she filled in their baby books the way she had diligently filled in Nikki's. It didn't seem fair to hang onto Nikki's baby things when she hadn't bothered to keep anything belonging to the others.

Not wanting to lose the shoes completely, she took a photo of them before she added them to the pile meant for the charity shop. She decided she would take photos of anything else that she didn't intend to hang onto but wanted to remember.

Despite looking forward to a new home and a new life in Picklewick, Beth would be sad to leave this house. Her children had been born here. Not in the house itself, of course – they had all been born in hospital – but this was where she had raised them. It held so many memories, some happy, some not so happy, and some downright horrid, but every single one was a piece of the mosaic that made up the picture of her life with her children.

If only they hadn't moved away...

But they had, and she wasn't prepared to rattle around in this house on her own, feeling lonely. She had four kids, one grandchild, and another on the way, and she hardly saw any of them. It simply wouldn't do. Which was why she had taken matters into her own hands and decided to be proactive, rather than sitting here feeling envious because all her friends had family living close by and she had no one.

Having sorted through the first few boxes, Beth took a break, and while she drank her mug of tea, she scrolled through the photos of the little terraced house in Picklewick and knew she was doing the right thing. She would be close enough to babysit Sammy or lend a hand when her daughters needed it, but not so close as to be living in anyone's pocket. She would be independent, yet still part of the family.

It would be perfect.

'Have you heard from Mum lately?' Dulcie asked. She was wiping the counters down as Maisie entered the kitchen. The aroma of freshly made cottage pie hung in the air, and Walter's tummy rumbled. It was nice not to have to cook for himself.

'Not for a few days. Why?' Maisie peered into the oven. 'That looks yummy.'

'I hope it tastes as good as it looks,' Dulcie said. 'Otto didn't make this, I did.'

'I'm sure it'll be delicious. You always were a better cook than me.'

'That's because you had Mum to cook for you.'

'I'm improving,' Maisie replied, 'But maybe I'll ask Otto for some pointers.'

'Best not, unless you want jus with this and jam with that,' Walter chortled. 'And I'm not referring to the kind of jam you can buy in the supermarket either. He was telling me about seaweed jam the other day. It sounded awful.'

Otto had also mentioned bourbon jam, which sounded much better. However, Walter didn't feel inclined to put it on his toast in the morning. How his son came up with these strange food combinations was beyond him.

Dulcie had finished tidying the kitchen and was now checking her phone. 'The last time I heard from Mum was nearly two weeks ago. It's not like her to maintain radio silence. How about you?'

Maisie peered at her mobile. 'About the same.' Her eyes widened. 'Do you think she's okay?'

'There's one way to find out.' Dulcie flicked a finger across the screen and waited for the call to be answered. 'Mum? Thank goodness! Are you alright?'

Walter could hear a tinny voice emanating from the phone, but he couldn't hear what Beth was saying, and neither did he want to. That woman was a damned nuisance.

After a couple of minutes the call ended, and Dulcie looked relieved. 'She hasn't rung because she's busy.'

'She could have messaged one of us,' Maisie said.

'Apparently she's too busy for that, too.'

'Why? What's she doing?'

'De-cluttering.'

Maisie frowned. 'I hope she isn't de-cluttering any of **my** stuff.'

'I thought you had fetched everything you wanted?'

'I did, but there's my old school reports and that project I did for art. Oh, and my cheerleading outfits.'

Dulcie laughed. 'I'd forgotten you used to do cheerleading. I bet Mum didn't keep any of them.'

'I put them in the attic.'

'They are probably still there, in that case. Mum hasn't been up there for years. I used to have to get the Christmas decorations down for her.'

'She won't be needing those again,' Maisie pointed out. 'Not if she spends Christmas here, like she did last year.'

Walter pulled a face. Beth had stayed at the farm for a full two weeks. **And** she'd turned up again at Easter. That visit had been for a couple of weeks, as well. She had every right to be here, considering she was Dulcie's mother, but Walter wished she wasn't so argumentative. Whenever he was in the same room as her, they seemed to butt heads. She was worse than his pet sheep, Flossie. Flossie was a head-butter too, but considerably less prickly. Beth called it, 'being forthright', and 'calling a spade a spade.' Walter called it annoying.

She was a fine-looking woman though, with her good cheekbones and her clear blue eyes, and when he'd first met her, he'd thought she was easy on the eye. It was a pity she wasn't equally as easy on the ear. Or his patience.

Maisie was saying, 'Isn't it daft how you never notice something, but when you do you see them everywhere.'

Dulcie replied, 'What do you mean? Another five minutes and I'll serve up, so do you want to lay the table?'

'Dalmatians,' Maisie said, getting a handful of knives and forks out of a drawer. 'I take it Otto's not eating with us?'

'Good lord, no! Do you think he'd let me cook if he was?'

'True. As I was saying, I saw a Dalmatian dog in the high street the other day, and now I keep seeing them everywhere.'

'Are you sure it's not the same one?'

'Don't say that, because I could have sworn I saw Mum's car in the village the other day too.'

'It's a well-known thing,' Walter said. He'd read about it recently. When the farm was his, he'd barely had time to open a newspaper, but these days he scoured it from end to end. What else did he have to do with his time? He continued, 'It's called 'the frequency illusion' where you see something, like a particular breed of dog or model of car let's say, or hear something like a name, and then you begin to notice it everywhere, so you think it's more common than it is.'

'You learn something new every day.' Dulcie opened the oven door and a waft of fragrant steam billowed out.

Walter's mouth watered. He was looking forward to this – good, simple, honest food, without any frills, just like his wife (God rest her soul) used to make. As so often happened when he thought of her, Walter was filled with sadness. She had died far too young, when Otto was a teenager. It was she who had nurtured Otto's love of cooking.

'I'll put some of this pie aside for Adam to have later, shall I?' Dulcie suggested, ladling out generous portions onto plates.

'That would be lovely, thanks.' Maisie gave her sister a one-armed hug.

It warmed Walter's heart to see how well the sisters got on, because that hadn't always been the case. Maisie had been drifting and rudderless when he'd first met her, flitting from job to job (Nikki used to call her Maisie Daydream), but the girl seemed to have settled down, helping Dulcie on the farm, as well as trying to get the old place on the hill up and running. She was a hard worker, he'd give her that, and so was Adam.

He envied the youngsters their enthusiasm, drive, and energy levels. Just thinking about it made him feel tired, but he supposed feeling tired was par for the course as one got older; and it hadn't helped matters that he had been so unwell. Thankfully, he could feel his energy slowly returning, although he was aware it would never be the same as it was.

He should learn to celebrate the small things, the little wins, such as he and Amos making play equipment for the goats, and him walking to the top of the mountain and back – even though it had laid him up for a couple of days afterwards.

Walter was feeling fine again now though, so maybe it was time to make inroads on all those odd jobs that needed doing around the cottage. If he took it slow and didn't over-exert himself, he was certain he could get them done without having to ask for help. It would give him something to do, and at the same time would prove to Otto and the rest that he wasn't over the hill just yet.

Despite the house looking barer than Beth could ever remember it being, the move to Picklewick still didn't seem real, even though she had given notice to her landlord, arranged for her post to be redirected, informed all the necessary utilities, and had booked the removal company.

It had been difficult to decide what she would take with her and what had to be got rid of (the house in Picklewick was smaller than this one, so about half of her furniture had to go), but afterwards she had felt strangely cleansed. And it hadn't taken as long as she'd anticipated to go through everything, and she was now left with the bare bones of her old home.

She had been quite ruthless and had probably thrown out stuff she could have used in her new place, but she wanted a fresh start; so this morning, with a week left until moving day, she intended to go shopping with Enka, who was probably her oldest friend. She had worked with her for almost twenty years until Enka had packed in her job to help look after her little grandson when his mum went back to work.

'What are you looking for?' Enka asked, as they walked towards the Bullring Shopping Centre, Enka dragging her shopping trolley behind her. Short and dumpy, Enka dressed like a Russian peasant from the nineteenth century and swore worse than a football hooligan. Beth adored her.

She was going to miss her badly, but they were seeing less and less of each other since both ladies had ceased work. Whereas Enka's life was full of her children and her grandchildren, Beth's life lacked both... Hopefully her move to Picklewick would rectify not seeing enough of her kids and Sammy.

Beth patted her handbag. 'Curtains,' she announced. 'I've brought the measurements with me. There are curtains up at the windows already, but they're not to my taste. And I thought I'd buy a couple of cushions to go with.' She beamed. 'I might even treat myself to some new tea towels.'

'I think you should,' Enka said. 'You can never have enough tea towels. Or flannels.'

'Shall we have a cuppa first?' Beth suggested.

If she was honest, she was keener on having a good old chin wag than buying curtains, because she was all too aware that it might be a long time before she saw Enka again. Once Beth was settled in Picklewick, she suspected she would be unlikely to return to Birmingham any time soon.

Cuppas bought, they settled themselves in a corner booth of the retro diner and Beth brought out a packet of Fig Rolls and offered one to Enka.

'I don't think you're allowed to eat your own food in here,' Enka said, taking one, nevertheless.

'I'm not paying those prices for a bit of cake,' Beth said, biting into hers. Fruity sweetness exploded on her tongue. 'Daylight robbery, that's what it is.'

'Will cake be any cheaper where you're going?' Enka asked.

'Doubt it. Nothing is cheap anymore.'

'What's Picklewick like?'

'Pretty, quiet, lots of fields around.'

'It sounds lovely.'

'It is. I'm not sure I'd want to live there if it wasn't for the girls, though.'

'Still, it's a fresh start, isn't it?' Enka helped herself to another Fig Roll and dunked it in her tea. 'You'll soon make new friends.' She arched a heavily pencilled eyebrow and added, '**Man** friends.'

'I don't think so. Not at my age.'

'You're never too old for a bit of how's-your-father,' Enka cackled. 'It puts a spring in your step.'

'I've got enough spring, thank you. Any more and I might as well have pogo sticks strapped to my legs.' Beth paused, her mug halfway to her mouth. 'You don't see many pogo sticks, these days, do you?'

 'You don't see many eligible men either – they're either serial bachelors or they're widowers and are looking for someone to wash their smalls.'

Beth chortled. 'You can say that again. I wouldn't have another man if you paid me.' The last one had left her with four kids, but at least he'd had the decency to pop his clogs before the divorce had gone through. Good riddance to bad rubbish, she always said.

But despite Enka's lamentations of there being no eligible men out there, it didn't stop Enka from looking. Beth was going to miss her friend's stories of her disastrous dates. They always made her chuckle. Where Enka found them was a mystery; Beth hadn't had a sniff of a date in years. Mind you, she didn't want to. At her age she was well past all that nonsense.

Love and romance were for the young – and they were welcome to it.

Drip, drip, drip... The damned noise was driving Walter insane. Every time it rained, it was like being tortured by the KGB. It was getting to the point where he began to dread seeing dark clouds gathering, and last night they'd gathered in abundance. Thankfully, the rain had held off until he'd managed to drop off to sleep, but when he'd woken in the middle of the night to use the loo, the incessant dripping had kept him awake.

The rain had stopped at around the same time as the sun had come up, but Walter knew that the dripping would continue for a while yet. Which was why he was at this moment trying to wrestle a set of ladders into position against the back wall of the cottage.

First, he would clear out the guttering, then he would scrape the moss away, before wrapping duct tape around the join between the two lengths.

As he shuffled the ladder slightly to the right, a drip landed on one of the metal rings and splashed into his face. Walter wiped it away with his sleeve, muttering to himself. At his feet, Peg whined anxiously.

'Don't worry, I haven't forgotten breakfast. We'll have tea and toast in a bit. I want to get this sorted first.'

The dog hung back warily, staying a safe distance from the ladder, and her brown eyes gazed worriedly at him. She disliked any change to her routine – unless that change involved a nice walk or an outing in the car. She had enjoyed the walk up to Maisie and Adam's place the other day, but like him, she'd been knackered afterwards. And, like him, the dog wasn't getting any younger.

With the ladder now in position, Walter gave it a little shake. It seemed steady enough. He wasn't keen on ladders, but this wasn't his first jaunt up one. He had done all his own repairs around the farm, apart from when the farmhouse had needed a new roof. About forty years ago, that had been, and he'd left it to a team of roofers because they knew what they were doing better than him. He was pleased that the roof was still going strong. Dulcie would probably get another forty years out of it before it needed replacing.

Taking a deep breath, Walter slid the roll of duct tape over his arm, and with a final check to make sure the ladder's base was level, he began to climb.

He had got about halfway up when his foot slipped, and Walter had a split second to lament the fact that he'd forgotten to change out of his slippers before he hit the ground with a sickening crack.

Walter wondered if he'd fallen asleep in front of the telly again as he struggled to open his eyes.

'Dad, can you hear me?'

Bloody hell, it was bright. Walter squinted, blinking as his eyes watered. Then he realised where he was, and as his memory came flooding back, his wince was equal parts pain and embarrassment.

Otto was peering at him anxiously. Walter struggled to sit up, but Otto put a hand on his shoulder.

'Do you know where you are?' his son asked.

'Of course I bloody know. I'm in hospital. I've broken my leg, not lost my marbles.'

'Just checking.'

'What time is it?'

'Why, have you got somewhere you need to be?'

'I haven't, but I bet you have.'

'I don't need to be anywhere else but here.'

'Liar.' Walter appreciated the sentiment though.

Otto sank onto a red plastic chair. 'What were you doing, going up a ladder at your age?'

'Cleaning out the gutters.'

'You should have asked me to do it.'

'Hmph. What's the time?' Walter repeated.

'Eight forty-seven.'

'Have you been here all day?'

'Yes.'

'You need to get off home.'

'I wanted to wait until they found you a bed.'

The ache in Walter's leg was abominable, and he shifted uncomfortably.

'They had to pin it,' Otto said.

'I know; they told me.'

'You'll have a cast for about six weeks.'

'They told me that, too.'

'How are you feeling?' Otto asked. He looked drawn and there were bags under his eyes.

Walter felt awful for worrying him. 'Not so bad.' His reply didn't fool Otto.

'Do you need any pain relief?'

'Aye, I could do with some.'

'I'll fetch a nurse.'

Walter closed his eyes. Not only was he in pain from his broken leg, but he felt sick, probably from the anaesthetic. His head was fuzzy, his memory jumbled. He remembered thinking, 'Oh shit,' followed by a terrible pain in his lower left leg. And he remembered Peg whining and licking his face. Then nothing until the ride in the ambulance and his arrival at hospital. More blurry memories; something about a CT scan and an X-ray, then being told he needed an operation.

He remembered feeling embarrassed because they cut his trousers off, and he recalled being asked to count backwards from ten. He also remembered asking someone to give Peg her toast, and lying flat on his back as he was being wheeled down a corridor, but he wasn't sure which order those memories were supposed to be in. He had a vague recollection of a firm female voice telling him to open his eyes, then more corridors, then being lifted into the bed he was currently in, before sleep reclaimed him.

His eyes must have drifted shut now, because he was startled by someone touching his wrist. 'Mr York, your son tells me you are a bit uncomfortable.' A nurse was peering at his chart and writing something down.

'You could say that,' he agreed.

'We'll get you something for your pain. Otherwise, how are you feeling?'

'Not so bad.'

'Not so good, more like,' Otto muttered. 'The daft sod.'

'Fell off a ladder, I heard,' the nurse said.

'He was wearing slippers.' Otto was shaking his head.

'We won't be doing that again, will we?' the nurse trilled.

'No, he bloody well won't. Will you, Dad?'

Walter pulled a face. 'I'll wear trainers next time. I forgot to—'

'I meant,' Otto broke in stonily, 'you won't be going up a ladder again.'

'But what about my guttering?'

'What about your waterworks?' the nurse asked. 'Do you need the toilet?'

Now that she'd mentioned it, Walter realised that he did need a pee. He also realised that it was going to be fun and games to get from the bed to the bathroom and back.

'Help me up,' he muttered to Otto.

The nurse said, 'No need. I'll get you a bedpan.'

'I'm not peeing into a bedpan. I'm not disabled.'

The nurse gave him a look. 'I think you'll find that is exactly what you are until your leg mends. You, Mr York, are going to need all the help you can get for a while.'

CHAPTER THREE

Beth was a bag of nerves. She should have said something before now. Well before. Like, when she had first thought of moving to Picklewick. Or when she had arranged to view her new house. Or when she'd signed the contract (which was the same day she'd been shown around it). Or any time since then. Even yesterday would have been good – better than today in fact, because today was moving day.

And none of her kids knew.

Her stomach was in knots at the thought of how they would react. Surely they would be pleased to have their old mum living close by? But this was Dulcie and

Maisie she was thinking of, and they mightn't be thrilled. Nikki wouldn't mind; Nikki was a different kettle of fish to the other two (Jay was different again, being a boy). Nikki was more like Beth in a lot of ways: straight talking, forthright, didn't suffer fools gladly. If she saw a problem, she'd want to fix it.

Maisie was a dreamer, a butterfly, flitting around without a care in the world. Beth had to hand it to Adam though, he'd grounded her youngest child, so there was hope for her yet. Dulcie sat between the two, personality wise and timewise. She would be the trickiest of the three to convince that Beth had made the right decision. Beth knew, without a modicum of doubt, that Dulcie loved her. But loving someone didn't mean you always got on, and Dulcie and Beth had often been at loggerheads when Dulcie lived at home.

A wave of guilt washed over her at the thought of 'home'. She was about to walk out of her kids' childhood home for the last time, and she hadn't given them the opportunity to say goodbye to it. What kind of mother did that make her?

After the removal men loaded the van, Beth walked around the house one last time. It was strangely upsetting to see it empty, as though its soul had dissipated, leaving a shell of the former happy home. Saying that though, Beth realised the house had lost its soul long before today. The soul had left it when Maisie had gone to Picklewick to live.

Beth set off for the village shortly after the removal van and, as she drove, her thoughts turned away from the house she had moved out of, and towards the one she was about to move into. She was looking forward to this new era in her life, with one exception – at what point did she announce her arrival to her girls?

She couldn't do it now obviously, because she was driving, and neither did she want to have that particular conversation over the phone if she pulled over into a layby. Better to do it face to face.

Or was it? A phone call would mean that she could tell them the news in as few words as possible and then end the call, thereby giving them time to process it before she saw them. Or would that be taking the coward's way out?

Probably, and no doubt Dulcie would hightail it into the village as soon as Beth put the phone down.

Oh dear, she really had got herself into a pickle, hadn't she?

Deciding to wait until her furniture had been unloaded because she couldn't deal with the removal men, Dulcie, and Maisie at the same time (Nikki would be at work, as this was a school day, and Beth didn't think it would be good for the poor pupils if Nikki got the news whilst she was in class), Beth carried on towards the village, mulling it over in her mind.

There was no option, she realised. She would have to tell them over the phone this evening. She would invite them to her new house, and although dealing with them en masse wasn't her preferred option, she knew she wouldn't have any choice, no matter which way she played it. As soon as she told one, the other two would know anyway.

Beth tried to put her dread to the back of her mind and concentrate on driving. The journey to Thornbury was on good A roads, but once past the town, the roads became narrower and twistier, and the chances of meeting a slow-moving tractor were greatly increased. So it was with slightly sweaty palms that she entered the outskirts of Picklewick, relief at arriving safely easing some of her tension.

She hadn't realised how stressful moving house could be, and that was without having to buy or sell a property. But she only had herself to blame for being even more stressed than she should be.

Hazelnut Road was just before the start of the high street proper, so she was hoping to park up without seeing anyone who knew her. Keeping her eyes peeled and feeling like a spy in a low-budget movie, Beth sank lower into the driving seat as she turned into the street where her cottage was situated.

Relief washed over her when she saw that the van had arrived, and she pulled into the kerb a short way beyond it. Clambering somewhat inelegantly out of her little red car, her back stiff and her knees protesting, Beth reached for her handbag.

'Won't be a sec,' she called to the men in the van. 'Just got to collect the keys.'

Beth took off down the road and hurried towards the estate agent, returning with the keys as fast as her legs could carry her. The removal men had opened the back of the van and were already manoeuvring her settee onto the raised platform.

Excitement fluttered in her chest. Beth was hardly able to believe that this lovely terraced cottage was to be her new home. It was considerably smaller than her house in Birmingham, but that was a bonus as far as she was concerned. Now that her last chick had flown the nest, two bedrooms and one reception room were plenty. And she loved the period features in this house. Nikki would probably say that it needed updating (it still had a back boiler behind the gas fire in the living room, and an airing cupboard and hot water tank in one of the bedrooms), but Beth thought it was perfect, and she particularly loved the built-in cupboards either side of the chimney breast. They were probably original, from when the house was first built, she thought happily, as she inserted the key into the lock and opened the front door.

But her happiness quickly evaporated, and she let out a cry of dismay.

The living room ceiling was all over the living room floor, and water was pouring through the hole.

Beth felt like crying and when one of the removal men said, 'Right love, where do you want this sofa?' she began to wail.

'I'm so sorry,' Zander, the young chap from the estate agent's office said, for the fifth time. 'You have my word that we'll get it repaired as soon as possible.'

'How soon?' Beth demanded. She felt sick. She had a van full of furniture, the house was inhabitable, and she was at her wits' end.

'We'll have to contact the landlord, obviously, and see whether they want to organise the repairs, or whether they'll want us to do it. And if so, we'll have to obtain quotes and—'

'So, it could be months?'

'Hopefully not that long. Thank goodness you had the presence of mind to turn off the water at the mains.'

'I didn't; one of the removal men did.'

The two men were currently sitting in the van, twiddling their thumbs. Beth could tell that they weren't amused.

'It prevented even more damage,' Zander said.

'Never mind that!' Beth cried. 'Where am I going to live?'

Zander paled. 'Oh, uh, well, I'll, um, have to check the landlord's insurance policy as to whether there's any contingencies built in for—'

Beth lost her patience. 'Don't bother. I'll stay with my daughter. Keep me updated as to when I can move back in. Not that I've actually moved in at all. And I don't expect you to chase me for rent when I'm not actually living there.'

'Of course not, Mrs Fairfax, although there may be—'

'Whatever you're about to say, don't.' Beth held up her hand. 'You've got a deposit and the first month's rent. You're not getting a penny more out of me until I've moved in.' That was the last word Beth intended to say on the matter.

She accompanied Zander to the door, locked it behind them, then handed him the keys.

'You've got my number,' she said, and marched over to the van.

The driver wound his window down. 'Where to, love?'

'Muddypuddle Lane. It's not far, just the other side of the village. You can follow me.'

Now I'm for it, she thought, as she got in her car and began to drive. She wasn't looking forward to the next couple of hours. Dulcie would be furious, and she had every right to be. Beth's life was going to be hell for a while. She just hoped that the repairs wouldn't take as long as she feared.

With the van tailing her, Beth drove slowly up the steep lane, wincing every time her little car encountered a pothole, and praying that her china wasn't being bounced around too much.

Bracing herself for a serious telling off, she turned into the yard, and didn't know whether to be relieved or disappointed when she saw that neither Dulcie's nor

Otto's car were there, and guessed that no one was home.

To make sure, she knocked on the farmhouse door and tried the handle. It was locked. Beth waved to the driver to wait a sec and made her way over to the barn.

Apart from the rabbits, it was empty of animals. Perfect.

'You can unload everything into the barn,' she told the driver.

It was the only logical place for her furniture to go. It was dry, and if Otto could dig out some plastic sheeting or tarpaulin, it should be safe enough until she was able to move it into her new house.

It took less time to unload than to load, and half an hour later Beth was waving them off. Wishing she had a nice cup of tea, she sat herself down on the settee to wait. There was little else she could do.

After the excitement of the day, Beth had fallen asleep. The barn was surprisingly warm and cosy, and her settee had always been comfortable, so she was disorientated when she woke to the sound of an engine pulling into the yard.

Blinking owlishly, she heaved herself off the sofa, feeling stiff and not quite with it, knowing that she needed to sharpen up if she was to survive the next few minutes. Peeping warily around the open barn door, she saw Dulcie get out of Otto's car, and heard her say, 'That's my mother's car. What is she doing here?'

Otto also got out, looking as handsome as ever. Dulcie had done alright for herself, Beth thought with pride. He was a good bloke, was Otto, and Beth was comforted by his presence. He wouldn't let Dulcie get too mad with her. Hopefully.

'Mum? Where are you?'

'In here.' Beth emerged slowly.

'What are you doing in the barn? Why didn't you tell us you were coming?'

Beth didn't move, and Dulcie walked towards her. It was only when Dulcie got near enough to see inside the barn that she stopped, and her eyes widened.

'Mum, what's all that?'

'My furniture.'

'Why is it in my barn?'

'I had nowhere else to put it.'

Dulcie's eyes widened even further. 'Please don't tell me you've been evicted.'

'I haven't been evicted.'

'Thank goodness! For a moment—' Dulcie stopped. 'What's going on?'

'I've got something to tell you, but can I have a wee first? And I'm dying for a cuppa. Got any cake, Otto?'

Wordlessly Dulcie opened the farmhouse door and gestured for Beth to go inside. As she hurried into the downstairs loo, she could hear her daughter and Otto having a hushed conversation, but despite putting her ear to the toilet door, she couldn't make out what was being said.

Nothing good, probably.

She was quite subdued when she entered the kitchen to find a teapot on the table and a slice of cake waiting for her. Despite her bravado, she didn't have much of an appetite.

Dulcie was leaning against the sink, her arms folded. 'Well?'

'I wanted it to be a surprise,' Beth began, 'but there was a leak in the hot water tank and the living room ceiling came down, and I had to go somewhere so I came here. My stuff will be alright in the barn, won't it? I thought if Otto could find some tarpaulin, he could cover it over.'

'Mum, you're not making sense. Are you trying to say that you've had a leak, and the ceiling has come down?'

'I'm not **trying** to say it – I **am** saying it. That's exactly what's happened.' Beth poured tea into a mug and took a grateful sip. She was parched.

'But you've not got a hot water tank. You've had a combi boiler for years.' Dulcie's expression was one of puzzlement.

'My new house has got a back boiler and a hot water tank.'

'Your new house? Have you moved?'

'Not quite. I was supposed to move in today, but when I got there, I found the ceiling on the floor and a great big puddle in the middle of the room.'

'Mum, that's awful! What does your landlord say?'

'It's through an estate agent, and they say they'll fix it, but it could be a while.'

'Have they offered you alternative accommodation?'

'No. I don't believe there is any.'

'Surely, they must have something on their books? They can't leave you homeless.'

'They've got to check the landlord's insurance policy, apparently.'

'How long will that take?'

'No idea. So, can I stay here?' Beth saw Dulcie and Otto exchange glances. Clearly having her stay with them, wasn't at the top of their wish list.

'Of course you can,' Dulcie said.

'My stuff will be okay in the barn, won't it?'

'It will, Beth,' Otto said. 'I'm sure I've got something to cover it over. Do you want a hand bringing anything in?'

'In a minute. I'll eat my cake first.' Her appetite was coming back. Dulcie wasn't as put out as Beth had feared. Mind you, Dulcie didn't know the whole story yet.

'Where are you moving to, Mum? I'm assuming it's somewhere smaller.'

'It definitely is.'

'Good for you. I've been saying for ages that the house is too big for you. Is that why you were having a clear out?'

Beth nodded, her mouth full of cake. She hoped she didn't look as shifty as she felt.

'Is your new house in Bournville?'

Beth inhaled sharply and a crumb went down the wrong way. Coughing until she was all hot and bothered, it took her a moment to catch her breath. When she had, Dulcie was still looking at her expectantly.

'Not exactly. It's in Picklewick,' Beth mumbled.

Dulcie was silent. Eventually she said, **'Where?'**

'Picklewick.'

'That's what I thought you said. The house you're renting is in **Picklewick?'**

'Yes.'

'Why?'

'I would have thought that was obvious. You're all here – except Jay. I miss you.'

'And you were supposed to be moving in today?'

'Yes.'

'When were you planning on telling us?' Dulcie's tone was frostier than the inside of a freezer.

'Today. This evening. When Nikki got home from school. I was going to ask if you'd like to pop in and see me.'

'You didn't think to mention it before now?'

'The time didn't seem right.'

'And you think **now** is the right time?'

'It wasn't supposed to happen like this.'

'I bet it wasn't.'

Beth got to her feet. 'I'll go get my cases.' There wasn't any point in continuing the conversation right now. She'd go to her room, have a lie down for a bit, and let Dulcie share the good news with her sisters. 'Am I in my usual bedroom?' she asked.

It was Dulcie's turn to look shifty. 'Not exactly.'

Beth winced as she heard her own words echoed back at her. 'Oh?'

Were they decorating? Or had Otto moved his office from the small fourth bedroom?

'You're in the bedroom at the back. The other is being used. Or it will be tomorrow.'

'By who?' Beth asked, her imagination running wild. She hoped the room wasn't being used because Maisie was moving back in. Beth had had such high hopes of Maisie and Adam's relationship working out. Such a shame.

'Walter.'

Walter? Wonderful! That was all she bloody needed.

'I can walk to the car,' Walter grumbled, as a nurse produced a wheelchair. He was supposed to sit in it for the journey from his hospital bed to the patient pick-up point outside the main door.

'Humour me,' the nurse said.

Walter inched his way forwards, turned slowly and sank into it with a grunt. He didn't want to admit it, but he was relieved that he wasn't expected to walk –

or should he say 'hobble' – out of the hospital. Even with Otto to carry his bag and Dulcie hovering beside him, just going from the bed to the wheelchair had exhausted him. And a trip to the bathroom laid him low for a good couple of hours.

That damned nurse had been right: he **was** going to need some help. Which was why he would be staying with Otto and Dulcie for the duration. He would have someone to cook his meals and do his laundry, and, more importantly, make sure he didn't fall down the stairs. Negotiating them, both up and down, was going to be interesting, and he had a feeling he might be using his bottom for both manoeuvres. It wouldn't be pretty or graceful, but it would be the safest way.

Dulcie had suggested that they bring one of the beds down and put it in the living room, but Walter had flatly refused. As long as he took his time, he would be able to negotiate the stairs twice a day. And the room Dulcie had decided to put him in was the one nearest to the bathroom, so he wouldn't have such a trek if he needed to go to the loo in the middle of the night. At his age if he only got up once for a pee, he considered himself fortunate.

Armed with a printed list of dos and don'ts, a small box of painkillers and an appointment to visit the fracture clinic, Walter left the hospital with a sense of relief.

'Where's Peg?' he asked as Otto went to fetch the car, leaving him and Dulcie to wait by the main doors.

'At the farm.'

'I was hoping you might have brought her with you. I've missed her.'

'She's missed you, too. She hasn't settled at all, bless her.'

'She's never left on her own,' Walter said. The dog had been his constant companion since he had been forced to give up the farm. And when Otto had moved out of the cottage on Muddypuddle Lane and had gone to live with Dulcie at the farm, Walter had been glad of her company.

'She's not on her own,' Dulcie told him. She hesitated, and Walter's heart sank. Don't tell me Maisie and Adam have had a falling out, he prayed silently. It was none of his business and he certainly wouldn't say anything, but they'd seemed so well suited.

'My mum is with her.'

'Eh?'

'My mother. She's come to stay for a while.'

Walter's mouth dropped open. He hadn't been expecting that. No one had mentioned anything about Beth coming for a visit. The last thing he needed when he wasn't feeling himself, was Dulcie's flippin' mother.

He tried to keep his tone neutral as he said, 'That's nice. Is she staying long?'

'A few weeks.'

Damn. 'Is everything alright?'

Dulcie rolled her eyes and sighed. 'Where Mum is concerned nothing is ever alright. To cut a long story short, she's decided to downsize and is moving into a smaller house. She was due to move in yesterday, but when she arrived at the property there had been a leak and one of the ceilings had come down. So she's staying with us until the house is repaired.'

Walter prayed it wouldn't take long; hopefully she'd be gone in a week or two and he could spend the rest of the time at the farm in peace, not seeing her again until her Christmas visit, which was a good few months away.

'There's more,' Dulcie said. 'The house she's supposed to be moving into is in

Picklewick. My mother is going to be living just down the road.'

Bloody marvellous, Walter thought. If anything was guaranteed to set his recovery back, it was that.

CHAPTER FOUR

Beth had made herself useful whilst Dulcie and Otto had been fetching Walter from the hospital. She had cleaned the kitchen, the downstairs loo, and the upstairs bathroom, and had put all her clothes away.

Eyeing the view from what was usually her bedroom but was now to be Walter's for the duration of his stay, she consoled herself with the knowledge that at least she could see up the mountain from the room she had been allocated. She couldn't see as far as Maisie and Adam's place, but it was a comfort knowing that her youngest child was just over the horizon.

During this time her phone had rung twice. The first call had been from Nikki, whose opening gambit had been a hissed, 'What the hell, Mum?' Apparently she'd heard the news, first from Dulcie who had sent her a message, then from Maisie who had tried to phone her when she had been in class and **then** sent her a message.

It seemed that Nikki wasn't pleased for two reasons. One, that Beth had kept it a secret ('You're as bad as Maisie. Scratch that, you're worse.') and two, because Maisie had phoned her during a lesson observation. Beth hadn't helped matters by telling Nikki that if she was so concerned about receiving calls, she should have turned her phone off.

The comment hadn't gone down well. Nikki had used her 'teacher voice' and had told Beth that she would see her later. It had sounded like a threat.

Maisie had accused Beth of being unable to cut the apron strings, and that she needed to let Maisie have a life of her own. Trust Maisie to make it all about **her**. Maisie clearly still had some growing up to do. The only person who was pleased that she had moved to Picklewick was her grandson. Sammy had sent her a message with one word in it – 'Wicked'. She briefly wondered what he was doing using his phone during school (she knew it was strictly against the school's policies), but she let it go. She needed all the support she could get, even if it was from an eleven-year-old.

Peg, Walter's gentle Border collie, also seemed pleased to see her and, after Dulcie and Otto had left for the hospital, the dog had followed her from room to room, as though Beth was a rather peculiar sheep that needed rounding up. Beth didn't mind. She appreciated the company, and it was one more 'person' on her side.

After she had done the chores, she made a cup of tea and sat at the kitchen table to await Walter's arrival.

Beth heard him before she saw him. As usual, he was grumbling, but she supposed this time he had good reason. She had never broken a bone in her life (but then, she hadn't been prone to going up ladders), but she could imagine how inconvenient it must be. Painful, too. She shuddered at the thought of the metal pin they'd inserted into Walter's leg, and wondered whether he would beep when he went through airport security, and if so, would the hospital issue him with some kind of letter to explain.

Beth sat up straighter when the kitchen door banged open, and Walter limped in, flanked by Dulcie. She had her hands outstretched, as though expecting to catch him if he toppled over.

Walter didn't say a word when he saw her, but his lips tightened and Beth guessed he was as unhappy to see her as she was to see him. Living in the same house as him was going to be a challenge, she thought, consoling herself with the hope that his stay at the farmhouse would only be for a few days. As soon as they could see that he could cope on his own, Dulcie and Otto would surely send him home.

Moving slowly, Walter headed for one of the kitchen chairs and lowered himself into it with much grunting and face pulling. His leg was sticking out, and Beth hoped no one would trip over it.

Peg, the traitorous creature, had been waiting patiently by the door, and was now nosing her master, asking to be fussed. So much for Beth thinking that Peg was on her side. Maybe she could get a dog of her own...?

Nah, it would need walking come rain or shine, and although Beth would be happy to take a dog for a walk when it was fine, she wouldn't be too keen on having to take it out when it was hammering down. And then there was the hair everywhere, and the dog poo that would need picking up. On second thoughts, maybe she would get a cat. Cats were far less trouble – maximum gain for minimum effort.

Whilst all this was going through her mind, she was studying Walter. He didn't look well. 'Drawn' was the best way to describe him. His cheeks were gaunt and his eyes had sunk, and the skin on his face was almost as grey as his hair.

Beth found herself feeling sorry for him. The fall and the subsequent operation had taken its toll.

'Let me get you a cup of tea,' Dulcie said. 'Here, give me your coat.'

Beth watched her daughter fussing around him and wondered whether she should play nice and offer to help. 'I'll make it,' she said, getting to her feet.

Otto had disappeared upstairs with Walter's bag, but he wasn't up there long and when he came back down Beth asked him if he also wanted a cup of tea.

'Not for me thanks. I'm going to the cottage to pack a few things for Dad. Anything in particular you want me to bring, Dad?'

Walter reeled off a list of things he couldn't live without, and Otto headed off, leaving Beth, Dulcie and Walter to make small talk.

Walter shot the opening volley. 'I can't believe you just turned up here out of the blue.'

Beth narrowed her eyes as she poured boiling water into the teapot. So that's how he was going to play it. 'I can't believe you were up a ladder at your age,' she retorted.

'Anyone hungry?' Dulcie asked.

'No,' Beth said.

'Yes.' That was from Walter. 'The food in that hospital was dire.'

Dulcie said, 'If you want something quick, I could heat up some soup or make you an omelette.'

'I don't want to put you out,' Walter said.

Beth returned fire. 'You should have thought of that before you went up a ladder. And in slippers, too.'

'It was an accident,' he shot back. 'Unlike what you did. You could hardly call moving house and not telling anyone an **accident**.'

'What I do is none of your business.' Beth's voice was sharp. How dare he lecture her on what she should or shouldn't do.

'Ditto.'

'Ooh, get you and your fancy words. Been looking up the crossword answers, have you?'

'Don't be so childish.'

'It's better than being oldish.'

'Oldish?'

'Yeah, too old to go up a ladder, and too stupid to realise it.'

'Mum!' Dulcie was aghast.

'It's true. Anyway, he started it.' Beth glared at Walter.

Walter glared back.

Beth had gained a lot of experience in outglaring teenage daughters, and she smirked when Walter looked away first. When she noticed that Dulcie was glaring at **her**, Beth quickly rearranged her features.

'I'm not standing for this, Mum. Walter needs rest; not you goading him. If you can't behave yourself, you'll have to go.'

Beth gasped. 'Where?' Surely Dulcie wouldn't throw her own mother out.

'Maisie's static has three bedrooms. You can stay there until your new house is repaired.'

'No!' Beth cried. Maisie would never agree. And even if she did, a static caravan would be too cramped for three.

Dulcie was still glaring. 'Promise me you'll behave yourself?' She had her hands on her hips and looked as though she meant it.

Beth forced out a reluctant, 'Yes'

'Good.' Dulcie turned her attention back to Walter, and Beth felt a small degree of satisfaction that Dulcie was going to berate him too.

But she didn't. When Dulcie said, 'What's it to be Walter, soup or omelette?' Beth ground her teeth together to hold her irritation in check.

The next couple of weeks were going to be very long indeed.

Bloody hell, this was going to be worse than he anticipated, and he wasn't referring to his broken leg, either. Walter was referring to Beth. Why, oh why, did she have to rock up at the exact same time he was incapacitated? And it looked like she'd already sharpened her knives and wasn't averse to stabbing him with them. Talk about kicking a man when he was down.

He held the moral high ground though: climbing a ladder to see to his guttering himself because he didn't want to bother Otto, might have been misguided but it had been done with the best of intentions. He couldn't say the same for the stunt that Beth had pulled. Deceitful and underhand, that's what she was. Although he did concede that she had a stroke of bad luck with her ceiling coming down. If she had been able to move into her house in the village today, her actions wouldn't have had such annoying consequences.

Poor Dulcie. Walter felt very sorry for her. Not only did she have him and his broken leg to contend with (which he was deeply sorry about) but she now had her mother to put up with. The woman was a menace.

Abruptly, he felt exhausted. All he wanted was to crawl into his own bed in his cottage and sleep for a week, but his cottage was out of the question. To his chagrin, he was acutely aware that he needed help (the nurse had been right) and the only way he would get it was to stay with Otto and Dulcie for a while. Otto, the poor boy, had too much on his plate with the restaurant to be able to give him a great deal of assistance, but Dulcie worked from home, so she'd be able to keep an eye on him. Walter hoped he wouldn't put her out too much.

'I think I'll go for a lie down,' he said as soon as Otto returned with his things, but as he tried to get up, he didn't know how. He feared putting any weight on his plastered leg, and he couldn't lever himself up using just the one.

Shuffling awkwardly to the edge of the chair, he reached for his crutches and promptly knocked them over. Dismayed and humiliated, he could feel his face flushing, and if he hadn't been so damned cross about the whole thing, he had a horrible suspicion that he might have burst into tears.

Quietly Otto bent to retrieve the crutches, holding them in one hand whilst he offered the other to Walter, who took it gratefully. But even with his son's help, Walter found it a struggle to get to his feet, and he was even more irate and embarrassed by the time he was upright.

Gritting his teeth and looking straight ahead, he limped out of the kitchen. Ungainly and awkward, he realised that using the crutches was going to take some practice. They hurt his arms, and even the short journey from the kitchen to the foot of the stairs left him with aching wrists and hands.

Panting with the effort, Walter gazed upwards in dismay. The thirteen steps might as well be a thousand. The thought of trying to heave his old carcass up them made him want to weep.

'I can't do it,' he muttered, leaning against the wall to try to take some of the weight off his good leg.

'No problem, Dad; if you can't get to the bed, we'll bring the bed to you.'

'I don't want to be a nuisance.'

'You're not a nuisance.' Otto put an arm around his shoulders.

'I'm sorry, son.'

'You've nothing to be sorry for.'

'I'm causing you nothing but trouble. It's not the first time you've had to bail me out.'

'Stop that right now. I'm not going to put up with you feeling sorry for yourself. Accidents happen.'

'I should never have gone up that ladder.'

'Too right you shouldn't, but what's done is done. Look on the bright side – it could have been a lot worse.'

Walter had been trying not to think about that.

Otto continued, 'Anyway, it'll only be for a few weeks. You'll be back on your feet in no time – excuse the pun. Let's get you into the living room, then I'll bring the bed down.'

Walter allowed himself to be guided into the lounge, where he sank gratefully onto the sofa with a grunt. Otto handed him the TV's remote control and gave his shoulder a squeeze before returning to the kitchen. Walter couldn't hear what was being said, but he could guess. Otto and Dulcie would be kind, he had no doubt. But he couldn't say the same for Beth. And even if she didn't say it aloud, she would be thinking it.

For the umpteenth time, Walter lamented that Beth was witnessing his frailty. He was a proud man (stubbornly so, Otto reckoned) and he hated her seeing him so helpless. It made him feel rather vulnerable, and the last person he wanted to show any weakness to was Beth Fairfax. Knowing her, she would take advantage and go for the jugular.

As he sat there, listening to the sound of Otto manoeuvring a bed across the landing, Walter wondered why he and Dulcie's mother didn't get on.

Ah, that was easy – she was annoying. But he didn't look too closely at why he found her annoying because it didn't matter. What mattered was that, aside from the next couple of weeks, he was going to see an awful lot more of her now that she would be living in Picklewick. He wouldn't simply be able to stroll up the lane and pop in to have a cuppa with Dulcie, because **she** might be there. And whenever Dulcie and Otto invited him for lunch or supper, in the interests of fairness they would have to invite her too.

For Walter, with Beth on the scene, life wouldn't be the same again.

What a palaver, Beth grumbled to herself, as she carefully crept down the steep stairs the following morning. It was incredibly early, but she had woken up to go to the loo and hadn't been able to go back to sleep. Typical.

She could have done with a couple hours more, because she'd been awake half the night. And that was Walter's fault. Twice she'd heard Otto go downstairs, presumably to check that the old man hadn't fallen out of bed. Or, worse, fallen over when he went to the bathroom.

The fuss if that had happened, didn't bear thinking about. Yesterday had been bad enough.

As Beth tiptoed through the dining room and into the kitchen (she didn't want to risk waking Walter), she pursed her lips as she remembered how Dulcie had fluffed pillows and smoothed the duvet before Otto had sent everyone out of the room so he could help his father change into his pyjamas to have a nap.

What was wrong with falling asleep in the chair like a normal pensioner, Beth wanted to know. She often napped in a chair, but she didn't feel the need to change into her nightie to do so.

Pouring boiling water into a mug, she mashed the tea bag against the side, then added milk, wincing at the rattle of the glass milk bottles as she closed the fridge door.

When she sat down at the kitchen table, she took a sip and grimaced. Ergh! Goat's milk! She had forgotten that was what Dulcie and Otto drank now, although they must have bought normal milk because she'd had a couple of proper cups of tea yesterday. No doubt the cow's milk would have been bought especially for Walter.

Beth, slightly ashamed of her uncharitable thoughts, tried not to feel bitter. If Dulcie had known she was coming, she was sure that Dulcie would also have stocked up on normal milk for her.

Recognising that some of her negative feelings regarding Walter stemmed from him living so close to the farm whilst she lived so far away, Beth resolved to try harder to be nicer to him. With her now living in the village (or she would be as soon as the repairs were done on her house) she had no reason to feel as resentful.

The remainder of her negative feelings were due to him simply being annoying. She had never met such an irritating man.

If she said the sun would come up tomorrow, he'd argue that it wouldn't.

She wondered how he was feeling this morning. Like a right idiot probably. What seventy-something bloke in his right mind would venture up a ladder whilst wearing slippers? He had been an accident waiting to happen.

Beth drank her tea and debated whether to poke her head around the door and ask if he'd like a cup. Then she decided against it, in case he needed the loo. She didn't mind making him a cuppa or fetching him something from the kitchen, but she drew the line at helping him to the bathroom, even if she didn't have to accompany him inside. And Walter seemed to need to go an awful lot. No sooner had he been helped into bed, he'd decided he needed the toilet, so Otto had to help him out of it and help him to get to the loo, then help him get back into bed. For Walter, a simple trip to the toilet involved an awful lot of helping, and right now Beth didn't feel up to it.

She suspected she never would.

However, in the interest of being nice (or **nicer**, at least) Beth vowed to help where she felt able.

Before too long, she heard someone stirring upstairs and shortly afterwards Dulcie appeared, bleary-eyed and yawning.

'I'm not going to ask if you had a good night,' Beth said, 'because I know you didn't. How many times did Walter get Otto out of bed?'

As soon as the words were out of her mouth, Beth could have kicked herself. So much for her vow to be nicer. But how could she be nice when her daughter looked exhausted?

Dulcie didn't reply; instead she asked, 'Do you want another cup of tea?'

Beth leapt to her feet, or as close to leaping as she got at her age. 'I'll make it. You sit down. Can I get you some breakfast?'

Dulcie shuddered. 'No thanks. Too early for me. I'll have something in a bit. Is Walter awake?'

'No idea.'

'I don't think I'll disturb him. We'll let him sleep, shall we? He needs his rest.'

What about me? Beth thought. **Don't I need my rest too?** She'd had a traumatic couple of days, what with the stress of moving and the subsequent disappointment. But when her inner voice told her to stop being so selfish, she had to admit it was justified. She **was** being selfish. Jealous, too, because Dulcie never showed **her** such concern.

It made her feel rather sad.

She didn't expect thanks for anything she'd done for her kids, but a bit of consideration now and again wouldn't go amiss.

Telling herself that things would pick up when she was living in her own house, Beth tried to look on the bright side: she could now see her girls whenever she wanted (within reason, of course), and she hoped to soon make friends in the village.

She could also be involved in the farm, because living in Picklewick meant that she would no longer feel left out. The fact that Walter would also be involved was a cross she would simply have to grin and bear.

'I can manage.' Walter sounded as cross as he felt, despite it being patently obvious that he wasn't able to manage the stairs without help.

Otto regarded him patiently, and Walter felt a stab of remorse. He ought not to be so grumpy, but he couldn't stop himself. He'd had a dreadful night's sleep, partly because his leg was giving him grief, partly because he hadn't been able to settle in a strange bed, and also because he kept fretting that he would need the loo and wouldn't get there in time.

It had taken him ages to heave himself out of bed and walk out the back to the downstairs bathroom, and that was **with** Otto's help. So he'd lain there worrying, until he'd worried himself into needing to go. Getting up once in the night was normal: three times was a damned nuisance. And it hadn't helped that Otto had kept coming downstairs to check on him.

Between one thing and another, Walter had only managed an hour's sleep here and an hour there.

He used his good leg and his arms to haul his backside onto the next step. Then he sat there for a couple of seconds, panting.

'Are you sure you won't have a shower?' Otto asked. 'We can wrap your cast in cling film and pop a bag over it.'

'I can't stand for long enough, can I?'

'I'm sure we can find something for you to sit on. A plastic garden chair perhaps?'

'It won't fit.'

'Something else then…'

'Like what?'

'I don't know. I'll have to have a think.'

'Don't take too long – I want a bath today, not next week,' Walter snapped. He knew he'd gone too far when Otto's eyes narrowed and his jaw clenched. Hastily, Walter attempted some damage control. None of this was Otto's fault, and it wasn't fair to take it out on him, especially since Otto was doing his best.

'I'll have a strip wash in the downstairs bathroom,' he said with a resigned sigh.

'Good idea.'

Walter eased himself down the stair he had hauled himself up just a moment ago, and struggled to his feet. His anger wasn't aimed at Otto; it was aimed at himself. What on earth had made him think he could climb a ladder at his age? Just look at where his idiocy had got him. Not only was he unable to have a bath or sleep in his own bed, he had to put up with Beth Fairfax to boot. She had a front row seat, and was currently sitting in the kitchen, smirking at his discomfort as he made his slow, awkward way to the loo, Otto hovering behind him, just in case.

Damn and blast her! The only way things could get any worse, was if Beth was the one who was accompanying him.

CHAPTER FIVE

Beth could have predicted Maisie's first words, so when her youngest cried, 'Mum! How could you!' she wasn't surprised.

'I thought you'd be pleased,' she said, knowing she was poking an angry wasp's nest but unable to help the sarcastic reply.

'You're joking, right?' Maisie gave her an incredulous look.

Beth tried not to show how hurt she felt. Maisie could at least pretend. Huffing, she stared out of the kitchen window. The kitchen was a nice enough place, but it wasn't where she would have wanted to spend the day. But with Walter hogging the living room, she didn't want to sit in there and have to listen to his sarcastic sniping. She wondered whether she should phone the estate agent and hurry them along. She hadn't been at the farm a day yet and already she was near the end of her tether. And Maisie wasn't helping.

'I can't believe you were going to move into a house in Picklewick without telling us,' Maisie continued. 'When did you arrange—?' She gasped and clapped a hand to her mouth. 'I **did** see your car in the village a couple of weeks ago! It wasn't the frequency effect, or whatever Walter called it.' She turned to Dulcie. 'I **knew** it was her car.'

Beth continued to stare out of the window, unable to think of anything to say in her defence. She was guilty as charged.

Maisie let out an exasperated sigh. 'Why didn't you discuss it with us first? Or at least, tell us what you were planning?'

'I wanted it to be a surprise.' Beth's voice was small. She really, really should have told them when the idea first came to her, but she had been too scared that they would have talked her out of it.

'It was a surprise alright,' Maisie grumbled. 'No wonder you've been busy **de-cluttering**.' She narrowed her eyes. 'What have you done with all my stuff?'

Beth was confused. 'What stuff? You took everything with you when you moved into the caravan. Your bedroom was empty, apart from three mouldy plates and a bed with broken slats. Did you use it as a trampoline?'

'My cheerleading stuff. It was in the attic.'

'It wasn't.' Beth was positive. 'I got rid of it years ago.'

'You didn't! I wanted to keep it.'

'Is that so? You haven't thought about it in years, have you?'

'No, but that doesn't alter the fact that I wanted to keep it.'

'I sold the whole lot, twirly baton and all, to a woman six doors down. The money I got for it paid for your school trip to Norfolk.'

'Oh, okay.' Maisie visibly deflated.

Beth had always made sure her kids never went without, and if that meant flogging a few bits and pieces, then that's what she did.

Dulcie hadn't said a word from the moment her sister had arrived, but now she said, 'Tea, Maisie? Before you see to the goats?'

Maisie nodded and took a seat at the table. 'Where will you be living?'

Some of Beth's tension eased. 'Hazelnut Road.'

'What's the house like?'

'Two up, two down, small garden. Living room ceiling currently on the living room floor.'

'So I heard. When will it be fixed?'

'Soon, I hope.' Beth hesitated. 'I won't be a nuisance, honest. I won't visit unless I'm invited.' She ignored Dulcie's snort. It wasn't Beth's fault that she felt the only way she would get to see her girls at Easter had been to rock up at the farm unannounced. If she'd waited for an invitation, she would still be waiting.

Dulcie put a fresh pot of tea in the centre of the table and got the milk out of the fridge.

'How's Walter?' Maisie asked, and Dulcie clapped a hand to her mouth.

'Oops, I'd forgotten Walter. Mum, do you mind asking him if he'd like a cuppa? And I don't think he's had any breakfast yet. Could you see what he wants? I've got to get on – I start work at nine, and Otto needs to be at the restaurant soon.'

Beth heaved a resigned sigh. She didn't relish running around after Walter, but if it helped Dulcie she would do it. At least Dulcie and Maisie didn't seem too cross with her now that they'd got over the initial shock. As long as she survived the next few weeks living in the same house as Walter, she had a feeling that moving to Picklewick might be the best thing she'd ever done.

Walter could hear voices coming from the kitchen and realised that Maisie was berating her mother. He didn't blame her. If he was Maisie, he'd be cross with Beth too.

But when his conscience reminded him that he had been no better when he'd hidden the farm's financial problems from

Otto, he felt a bit guilty for being so judgemental. He had acted far worse, hiding the situation for months, until the stress had put him in hospital and forced Otto to give up his lucrative job as one of London's top chefs.

So Walter honestly didn't have a leg to stand on. Beth relocating to Picklewick without informing her family was small fry compared to what he had done. Maybe he should cut her some slack.

But cutting her some slack didn't make her any less irritating or abrasive. She rubbed him up the wrong way, and he suspected he did the same for her. Speak of the devil…

Beth's face appeared around the living room door. 'Tea? And Dulcie wants to know what you want for breakfast.'

'I'll have a cup, if there's one in the pot. But tell her not to bother with breakfast. I can make my own.'

'Pft! How are you going to do that without any hands?'

'I've got hands.' He waved them in the air. 'See?' Was she really as daft as she sounded?

'They'll be holding onto your crutches,' she told him.

She had a point. 'Other people manage.' He wasn't sure how, but they must do.

'If you think you can fry yourself an egg, be my guest.'

'I don't want a fried egg.'

'What **do** you want?'

'Toast.'

'One slice or two?'

'Two, but I can do it myself.'

'Dulcie keeps her toaster in the cupboard next to the sink. Good luck with bending down to get that out and don't blame me if you fall over.'

'I won't fall over.'

'Look—' She moved further into the room and put her hands on her hips. 'Stop being such a stubborn old git and let me make you some toast. It's no bother. It'll be more bother if you fall and break your other leg.'

'I won't fall,' he repeated. She was right though; until he got the hang of those crutches, he was a danger to himself. It didn't help that he felt as weak as a kitten and utterly exhausted. 'Not too much butter, and a dab of marmalade wouldn't go amiss,' he relented.

'There, that wasn't so hard, was it?'

Actually, it had been torture admitting, even tacitly, that he needed help from Beth. At least he was out of bed and dressed (thanks to Otto), which made him feel less of a patient and more of a guest.

Beth returned a few minutes later with a plate of hot, buttered toast and a mug of tea. Thankfully she didn't decide to keep him company, so he ate his breakfast in peace whilst watching morning TV. But eventually he needed the loo and the thought of Beth's eyes on him as he made his way through the kitchen, got him cross all over again.

Before that though, he had to get out of the chair. Determined not to call for help, he shuffled his bottom closer to the edge of the seat and positioned his good foot as near to the chair as possible. It took him three goes before he managed to get to his feet, and by the time he was upright sweat was beading his brow and trickling down his back. But he'd done it!

Unfortunately that was where it fell apart. As he reached for his crutches, he managed to knock them over. They fell to the floor with a clatter which brought Dulcie and Beth running.

Dulcie got to him first, bending down to pick them up. She held onto his elbow to steady him, as he slid his arms into them.

'You get back to work,' Beth told Dulcie. 'I'll sort Walter out.'

'I don't need sorting.'

'I think you'll find you do.'

Yeah, he could guess what kind of sorting she would like to do to him.

With the crutches in position, he hopped forwards, his progress slow and hesitant. Despite the rubber ends, Walter was scared they would slip and he'd fall, as Beth had predicted. Now that she'd put the idea in his head, he couldn't shift it. Thanks, Beth.

As he gingerly hopped and swung his way through the dining room, he was all too aware of Beth inches from his elbow, ready to catch him should the worst happen. What use would she be if he did topple over, was anyone's guess. He was more likely to take her down with him and Dulcie would then have two patients on her hands, not one.

'No need to stand so close,' he hissed. Dulcie was on a call, headphones on, her eyes focused on the computer screen.

'There's no point in me being four feet away, is there?'

She was so close Walter could smell her perfume. Or maybe it was her shampoo or the washing powder she used. Whatever it was, he liked it.

Dulcie shot them a look and put her finger to her lips.

'I don't need you to accompany me to the toilet,' Walter insisted.

'Don't be stubborn. Otto had to take you this morning.'

'That's because I wasn't used to the crutches.'

'And you are **now**?' Beth sounded incredulous.

'I'm getting the hang of them,' he insisted.

'Shh!' Dulcie was frowning and shaking her head.

Beth said, 'Get a move on, you're disturbing Dulcie.'

'I'm going as fast as I can. And you're the one who's disturbing her, not me.'

'Excuse me, for a second,' Dulcie said, and removed her headphones. 'Do you mind? I'm trying to deal with a customer complaint here.'

'See?' Walter hissed. 'I told you that you're disturbing her.'

Dulcie huffed. 'It's both of you. Please keep the noise down. If you want to bicker, do it in the living room – quietly.'

'I don't want to bicker,' Beth said. 'He started it.'

'You sound like Sammy,' Walter retorted.

'Better than sounding like a miserable old codger.'

'I'm only miserable because you make me miserable.'

'Mum! Walter! **Stop it.** If you don't keep the noise down, I swear I'll go and work at the restaurant and leave the pair of you to slug it out on your own.'

Walter was immediately contrite. 'Sorry, Dulcie.' He stared at Beth, who glared stonily at him before adding her own apology.

Walter carried on walking (if you could call it walking) and managed to get as far as the bathroom without pausing. Once inside, he bolted the door and leant against it.

His shoulders were sore, his arms were aching, and so was his good leg. Being injured was no joke when you were his age, and he briefly wished he had accepted the hospital's offer to refer him for assessment for a wheelchair. But, then again, he would never get a wheelchair through the farmhouse's narrow doorways.

There was nothing for it, he would have to get used to the crutches. Short dabs, every so often, would give him a bit of practice without overdoing it. But right now, making it to the loo and back was practice enough. Maybe he'd feel a bit stronger tomorrow.

And maybe pigs might fly. He was kidding himself if he thought he would bounce back in a matter of days. It was going to take a couple of weeks. He hated having to admit it, but the fall and the operation had taken it out of him, and he felt he was almost back to where he'd started when he'd suffered the collapse last year.

Almost, but not quite. Mentally, he was much stronger than he had been, and he had Otto and Dulcie to thank for that. His broken leg was a setback, that was all, and once it was mended he would soon be back to his old self. He'd learnt his lesson though – no more climbing ladders.

But if he couldn't keep busy with DIY, he would have to find something else to occupy him, otherwise he would go mad with boredom. And although he had Peg to keep him company, he was often lonely. He just wished he knew what he could do about it.

Beth hated being at a loose end, but with the living room being out of bounds (there was no way Beth was going to join Walter to watch the nonsense that was on daytime telly), and with Dulcie needing peace and quiet in the dining room, Beth didn't know what to do with herself.

If she had been in her own house, she would have run the vacuum cleaner round and done a bit of dusting, but knowing that she mustn't make too much noise, she satisfied herself with giving the kitchen the once over (despite it being spotless) and bleaching the downstairs bathroom. Then she made yet another cup of tea. If she drank any more of the stuff, she'd need to use the loo as much as Walter; although she strongly suspected he was only doing it to wind her up.

Unable to sit still any longer, Beth rinsed out her mug and went outside. She would check on her furniture, then maybe she would go for a stroll.

True to his word, Otto, the dear boy, had found some tarpaulin and a length of plastic, and had covered all her bits and pieces. Thankfully, the barn was dry and there was no rain forecast, so she needn't worry. And with any luck, she would be moving into her own home before too long.

She spent a few minutes watching the rabbits hop around their runs, and even stroked a soft ear or two. Then she wandered over towards the goats' field. But before she got there she bumped into Maisie, who was coming out of the pasteurisation shed. She had Peg with her, and Beth was flattered when the dog greeted her like a long-lost friend.

'She's really taken to you,' Maisie observed. 'I didn't think you liked dogs.'

'Because we never had one when you were a kid?'

'We didn't have any pets.'

'There was a good reason for that. Looking after you lot was enough.'

'I would have helped.'

Beth raised her eyebrows.

'Okay, maybe I wouldn't have helped as much as I thought I would.'

'You wouldn't have helped at all. None of you would. You'd have made all the right noises in the beginning, but after a couple of weeks it would have fallen on me to look after it.'

Maisie gave her an apologetic look. 'You're probably right.'

'I know I am.'

'I'm sorry I gave you such a hard time earlier. But you've got to admit, turning up with all your worldly possessions yesterday was a bit of a shock.'

Beth bit her lip. 'It was more of a shock for Dulcie.'

'And Walter,' Maisie added, with a grin. 'I wasn't expecting him to be here.'

'Neither was he. From what Otto told me, his dad had expected to go home and pick up where he left off. But at his age, a broken leg isn't something you can shake off easily.'

'Don't you mean at **your** age?' Maisie teased. 'He's only a year or so older than you.'

'Four, actually, and thanks for reminding me.'

'You don't look your age,' Maisie said.

'Flatterer. What do you want?'

'Take Peg for a walk for me?'

'I might have known.'

'Please? I promised Walter.'

'Oh, well, if you promised **Walter.**'

'Don't be so mean. He would take her himself if he could.'

Beth knew Maisie was right. Walter worshipped that dog. 'Go on then,' she said. 'I'll take her down the lane for a stroll.'

'Thanks, Mum. It means I can get on with soap making.' She looked hopeful. 'You could always give me a hand with that, if you like?'

'No thanks! I'll stick to taking Peg for a walk.'

Beth called the dog to her and had just turned away when Maisie asked, 'What have you got against Walter, anyway?'

Beth didn't answer, because she didn't honestly know.

Beth looked at the pained expression on Walter's face as he thanked her for taking Peg for a walk.

'You're welcome,' she said sweetly. 'Peg's a poppet.' Unlike her owner, she thought, but didn't say.

'How far did you go?'

'Only down the lane and back.' Beth helped herself to the mashed potato she had cooked for everyone's tea. And by 'everyone' she meant herself, Dulcie and Walter, because Otto was at the restaurant. If he hadn't been, he wouldn't have allowed her anywhere near the stove.

Beth had enjoyed feeling useful though, and seeing the way Dulcie and Walter were devouring their food, she assumed she hadn't done too bad a job. It was rather tasty, she thought; gravy made with the juice from the sausages and from frying onions was a taste sensation. She'd added a bit of swede to the mash, and was serving carrots and peas with it.

'I bumped into Lena. She was asking after you, Walter. She says to tell you that Amos will pop up to see you in a couple of days.' Beth had met Lena, Amos's other half, a couple of times and liked her immensely. It would be nice to have another woman of roughly the same age around, and Beth was hoping that Lena would carry through her suggestion of, 'You must pop in for a coffee when you're settled.' She fully intended to throw herself into village life and make as many friends as she could.

Walter muttered, 'I don't want him to see me like this.'

'Like what?' Beth asked. She genuinely wanted to know. People broke bones every day – what was so special about Walter's broken leg?

'Helpless,' Walter replied.

'Hopeless, more like,' Beth muttered under her breath, earning herself a sharp look from her daughter.

'You're not helpless,' Dulcie said in a no-nonsense tone.

'What do you call it then?'

'A little less able than usual.'

Walter snorted. 'A lot less.'

'You managed to get out of the chair by yourself a couple of times this afternoon, and you're walking so much better on your crutches.'

'I still can't get upstairs by myself,' he grumbled. 'I want my own bed. I don't like sleeping downstairs; it's not natural.'

'It's unavoidable,' Dulcie soothed. 'And it'll only be for a few weeks.'

'I bet I could manage my own stairs. They're nowhere near as steep as yours. I'd be able to have a bath, too.'

Dulcie put her knife and fork down and looked him square in the eye. 'Walter, you can't go home just yet. You know that.'

'I bet I could.'

'You couldn't even make yourself some toast this morning,' she pointed out.

This is like being at Wimbledon, Beth thought. She'd never been and didn't want to, but she'd seen enough clips on the telly of people swivelling their heads from side to side as they followed the ball, and Beth was doing the same thing. She wondered who would win. Her money was on Dulcie, if only because Walter would need a lift to his cottage: he would never make it down the hill on his own.

A wicked thought entered her head. Perhaps she could offer to take him home? Then she hurriedly dismissed it. Dulcie would never forgive her, and neither would Otto. Besides, if anything bad were to happen to Walter because he'd returned home before he was able to look after himself properly, she wouldn't forgive herself either. He might be a royal pain in the backside, but she didn't want any harm to come to him.

Walter growled, '**She—**' He jabbed his fork in Beth's direction, and Beth flinched. 'Didn't give me the opportunity to find out.'

'Have a go now, why don't you?' Beth glared at him.

'I will, after I've finished my tea.' He jabbed the fork into a piece of sausage and shovelled it into his mouth, then chewed vigorously.

'Look, Walter,' Dulcie said. 'We're not being deliberately awkward. We care about you, and we want to make sure you can cope on your own before we take you home.'

He sighed, pushing his empty plate away. Having a broken leg and being cross about it hadn't affected his appetite, Beth noticed. She was pleased he'd enjoyed her cooking, though.

He said, 'I know you care, but I need to be in my own home.'

'This used to be your home, can't it be your home again for the time being?'

'No. It's yours and Otto's.' His voice was firm. 'It's not mine. There's been too many changes.'

'Oh, Walter, I'm so sorry.' Beth saw that Dulcie had tears in her eyes.

He said, 'You've nothing to be sorry for. It's only natural you wanted to make the place yours.'

'It's yours, too, Walter. It always will be.'

'That's where you're wrong, my lovely girl. My house is the cottage down the lane now. And I want to return to it.'

'Walter, I—'

He slapped his palm down on the table, making Beth jump. 'Damn it, Dulcie, I'm old enough and ugly enough to know what's best for me.'

Beth snorted, disagreeing with both parts of that statement. Old didn't necessarily mean wise, or even sensible. And he certainly wasn't ugly. He wasn't bad looking at all, despite his face being on the rugged side. It must be from all those years working outdoors.

'What you need is a housekeeper,' Beth said.

'Are you offering?'

'Not likely. I couldn't think of anything worse than listening to you carping, like you did today. On and on, grizzle, grizzle, moan, moan.'

Dulcie was staring at her, her gaze intense.

'What?' Beth demanded.

'Mum, you're a genius.'

'I am?'

'Hear me out,' Dulcie began, and Beth's spirits sank. Nothing good ever followed those three little words. Dulcie said, 'Being Walter's housekeeper is a great idea. He would be happier, and you would be doing Otto and me a massive favour.'

Beth was shaking her head. 'No, definitely not. No way!' Could she be any clearer? 'Over my dead body.'

'That could be arranged,' Walter muttered. 'There is no way that woman is staying in my house.'

Dulcie smiled at him. 'Even if it means you can stay there too?'

'Don't I get any say in this?' Beth demanded hotly.

'Of course you do. If you don't feel you can look after Walter in his own house, you can help look after him here. But can you keep the noise down when you're doing it? One of my callers thought there was a domestic going on and asked if they should call the police.'

Beth glowered at her. Hadn't she been helping already? And what thanks had Walter given her? None, that's what. He'd done nothing but complain, and whine, and and—

An idea struck her. Walter in his own home would be a less miserable Walter. If he stayed here he would continue to gripe, and she didn't think she could face another day of him carping. And once he was back in his cottage, she would do her utmost to convince Dulcie and Otto that he could manage on his own. Then she could move back into the farmhouse and enjoy some peace and quiet until her house was ready for her.

The surprise on Walter's face when she said, 'Okay, I'll do it,' was the highlight of her day.

CHAPTER SIX

On the one hand, it was a relief to be in his own home. On the other, Walter was in it with Beth. He didn't know whether to laugh or weep, and was hovering on the verge of hysteria despite having been home for only a couple of hours.

Walter had wanted to leave the farmhouse immediately after he'd finished his sausage and mash (he would say that for Beth, she was a decent cook), but Dulcie had refused. In the end, he'd stayed there another night, and Otto had brought him and Beth to the cottage this morning.

His son hadn't been happy about it, but he'd not been able to put up much of an argument considering Beth was going to be staying here with him. How long, remained to be seen. If Walter had his way, she would be gone by the end of the week. All he had to do was to prove that he could make himself a sandwich and wasn't in danger of falling over when he put his trousers on.

Beth would be sleeping in Otto's old room, and he could hear her pottering around in there now. She had brought a case with her, but he hoped she wasn't bothering to unpack it, as she would only have to repack it in a day or so.

Anxious to prove that he didn't need her help, Walter eased himself into the kitchen, Peg close behind.

The collie seemed equally as happy to be home, although the traitorous little madam seemed just as happy to have Beth here. He was sure that Peg would soon change her mind the first time Beth yelled at her – which was bound to happen. Beth didn't strike him as much of a dog lover, and she had yet to experience the joys of picking up poop or bathing a dog who had rolled in something nasty.

Walter leant a crutch against the fridge door and used his free hand to remove the milk. A careful swivel and he was able to put the bottle on the counter. Pleased with his progress so far, he carried on with his tea-making, remembering to retrieve the crutch. So far, so good.

Then he realised he wouldn't be able to carry his mug into the living room, because he hadn't yet mastered being able to walk with just one crutch. Which meant that until he did, he would either have to eat and drink standing in the kitchen, or rely on someone (Beth) to carry it in for him.

Beth came downstairs at the exact moment he decided to give simultaneous tea-carrying and walking on one crutch a go, and managed to slop it everywhere. To his chagrin, she didn't notice the wet floor and stepped in the little puddle. Her foot skidded, her leg went from under her, and she almost fell.

Righting herself, she glared at him, taking everything in with one scornful glance. 'What are you doing?' she demanded. 'I could have broken my neck, you silly man.'

She snatched the mug out of his hand, spilling the rest of the tea, and put it down on the countertop with more force than was necessary.

Walter winced. 'I was making tea.'

'Making a mess, more like.' She tore off a couple of sheets of kitchen roll and bent to mop up the spill.

Walter glared at the top of her head, feeling useless. He couldn't even make a cup of tea without incident, so what hope did he have of preparing a meal?

Then he told himself off for being so negative. He could have drunk it standing in the kitchen, and if he had, he wouldn't have spilt it. However, standing for more than a few minutes made his good leg ache, but the way around that was to ask Beth to bring one of the dining chairs into the kitchen. Problem solved!

Mostly.

Eating his dinner whilst balancing a plate on his knee wouldn't be easy, (the chair wasn't high enough to be able to eat at the worktop), but he was sure there must be a tray around here somewhere. And if not, Beth could pop into the village and buy him one.

Beth straightened up and put the sodden kitchen roll in the bin. 'Go sit down, you daft old sod. I'll fetch you a cup of tea.'

'Can you bring a chair into the kitchen first?'

She didn't move. 'What's the magic word?'

'Eh?'

'Haven't you got **any** manners?'

'Oh, I see. *Please*.' His sarcastic emphasis didn't go unnoticed, but he ignored her arched brow. A momentary standoff ensued, but Beth gave in first and went to fetch the chair.

'Where shall I put it?'

He pointed to a corner. 'There will be good.'

Plonking it down, she said, 'What do you want it for, anyway?'

When he explained and she nodded to show she understood, he knew they were on the same page: she wanted him to be self-sufficient as much as he.

It was lunchtime and Beth was hungry. Walter must be too, but she couldn't work out how to use this blimmin' oven. It had taken her long enough to realise that there wasn't a kettle, and that the curved tap beside the sink dispensed boiling water as well as ice cold.

Otto's doing, she surmised. He liked his gadgets, being a chef, but all she hoped was that she wasn't expected to use any of them.

Giving up on the stove for the time being, she decided to make them both a sandwich, then she'd work out what they could have for their tea, and if she needed to go shopping she could pop into the village.

She also wanted to give the cottage a good clean. On the surface it was tidy and looked clean enough, but it wasn't up to Beth's standards and if she was to live here for a few days, she didn't intend to live in muck.

Well, what could you expect from an old chap who lived on his own, she mused as she bustled to and from the fridge, taking out the makings of a cheese and pickle sandwich. She was pleased to see that he used real butter, not the chemical-infused rubbish that the supermarkets tried to pass off as butter. And he had proper milk too, although the date was up today, so she would have to buy more soon. The bread wasn't as fresh as she liked, either. She would go shopping tomorrow, she decided. Today she would clean.

Sandwiches made, she took them into the living room and placed them on the table. The two of them ate in silence, Walter sneaking Peg the odd morsel, and Beth made a note to remember to turn the telly on in future. Mindless daytime TV would be better than listening to Walter chewing.

He did manage to force out a 'thank you' after he'd finished eating, so that was something. Her sarcastic, 'You're welcome,' earned her a sharp look.

Leaving Walter to his crossword puzzle, she took the empty plates into the kitchen and began to clean up. After about half an hour, during which Beth had run several bowlfuls of hot water and had cleaned out most of the cupboards, she became aware that she was being watched.

Walter looked thunderous. 'What are you doing?' he demanded.

Beth was on her hands and knees, the contents of his saucepan cupboard spread out on the floor around her, scrubbing vigorously at a rusty mark marring the white melamine shelf.

'Ballet dancing. What does it look like I'm doing?'

'Interfering.'

'Somebody has to. This place is a disgrace.'

'I find that offensive.'

'Yeah, so do I – that's why I'm giving everything a good wipe over.'

'Unbelievable. I thought you were here to help. Peg needs a walk and Flossie, Princess and Toffee need checking.'

'I'm not your servant, you know,' Beth retorted. The cheek of the man! She was doing her best to help and he was ordering her around. 'Fine.'

She gathered the pans together and shoved them noisily back into the cupboard. The clatter brought Peg running into the kitchen, barking loudly.

'Now see what you've done,' Walter said. 'You've frightened my dog.'

Peg didn't look frightened, but Beth was instantly repentant. The poor creature had enough to put up with having Walter as her owner; she didn't need Beth scaring the living daylights out of her.

Beth stomped into the hall to fetch her shoes and as she was putting them on, she said, 'What am I supposed to be checking?' Beth had seen Walter's pet sheep and the two goats belonging to the stables, from the window. They looked fine.

'I always checked my flock every morning.'

'Yes, but what did you check **for?**'

'That none were injured or ailing, that one of them hadn't got caught in a fence, that they weren't having difficulty lambing...'

Beth was horrified. '**Lambing?**'

'It was an example. None of them are pregnant. It's the wrong time of year.'

'Why mention it?'

'As I said, it was an example.'

'I don't need to check: they look fine. None of them are caught in a fence.'

'How about limping?'

'The only thing limping around here is you.'

He pursed his lips. 'Very funny. Can you check anyway? They might need their feet looking at.'

Beth put her hands on her hips. 'I am **not** looking at their feet.'

'I don't expect you to. Amos or Petra will see to it.'

'So why don't you ask **them** to check the animals?'

'They're busy.'

'And I'm not?'

'No, you're interfering.'

'We're back to that, are we? Come on Peg, let's go for a walk and leave your ungrateful master to stew in his own juice.'

Honestly, some people! She would have thought he'd be glad to be back in his own house, being waited on hand, foot and finger. But no... all he could do was sit there with a sour expression on his face and berate her for trying to help.

Sod him. If he wanted to live in muck, then so be it. She would do the minimum necessary until he could cope on his own, and then she was out of here.

'Blinkin' heck,' Walter muttered as he opened first one cupboard, and then another. That damned woman had rearranged all of them. Where the hell were the tea bags?

He found them in the same cupboard that the coffee was in, which might seem logical to her, but it was the cupboard furthest away from the magic tap. He knew that wasn't the correct name for the tap that spat out both boiling and freezing water, but he'd joked with Otto that it was magic when Otto had renovated the kitchen prior to Walter and Otto moving in, and the name had stuck.

The tea bags should live on the shelf underneath it. As should the mugs, which were now in the cupboard with the plates.

Hopping awkwardly and cursing as he went, he put his cupboards back the way they were. And if she moved any of his stuff again he wouldn't be accountable for his actions.

As he popped a tea bag in a mug, movement beyond the kitchen window caught his attention.

A woman was sitting on the topmost rung of the gate leading to the paddock. She was swinging her legs, her face turned away as she gazed into the field. For a moment he couldn't place her and he wondered whether she was one of the riding school mums. Then it hit him.

The woman was **Beth.**

His breath lodged in his throat and he feared he was hallucinating because she looked years younger, and he caught a glimpse of how she must have once looked: vibrant, carefree, not yet weighed down by time and age.

Then his focus sharpened, and she was Beth Fairfax again: pensioner, cantankerous, disagreeable.

She must have been striking once though. And as she sat there, her face lifted to the sun, he could see a younger version, one that had echoes of her beautiful daughters etched on her face. Walter, despite his dislike, had to admit (as he had done previously) that she was still a handsome woman. If only she wasn't so difficult and obstinate...

Walter paused, wondering where he was going with that thought, but the destination eluded him.

Whatever fanciful notion she had generated in him, swiftly disappeared when he watched her clamber gracelessly down from the five-bar gate. His heart was in his mouth. If she were to fall... And she had the cheek to accuse him of being silly when he'd gone up the ladder! She was just as bad. One slip of the foot and she could have broken her hip.

Irritated at her carelessness, he hobbled to the back door as fast as his cast would allow and yanked it open. 'What the hell do you think you're doing?' he bellowed, feeling rather satisfied when he saw her startled expression.

'Checking this lot,' she called. 'You asked me to. Don't you remember?' She began walking towards him. 'Or is your memory going?'

'I didn't ask you to climb a bloody gate,' he yelled back. 'And my memory is fine.'

'I was enjoying the sun. Or is that not allowed?'

'Don't be so silly.'

'Who are you calling silly?' She was close enough to see the flash of anger in her eyes.

He said, 'You, obviously. You could have fallen.'

'So says Spider Man. You're the one who fell, not me!'

She was daring him to contradict her. 'Which is why I know what I'm talking about. Breaking a hip is no laughing matter.'

'You didn't break a hip. Are you sure you're not losing your memory?'

'You could have broken yours.'

'But I didn't.'

'Gah! There's no talking to you!'

'Don't, then. See if I care. I'm fed up with you bumping your gums.'

'And I'm fed up of everything about **you!**' Walter yelled.

He liked to think that he whirled on his heel and marched inside, but what actually happened was that he did an awkward shuffling about turn, involved hopping, then limped slowly indoors.

He could feel Peg booping him on the leg in concern, and he guessed that the dog mightn't be getting her walk after all as Beth stomped in behind him and reached for the handbag that she'd looped over the back of one of the dining chairs.

'I'm going out,' she announced.

'Where?'

'Shopping. Your milk is off, and your bread is stale.'

'The milk seemed alright to me.'

'It would,' she growled. 'If I said it was white, you'd argue that it was blue.'

'What are you rabbiting on about?'

'Can I get you anything? A gag? A sedative? Some manners?'

Walter stared at her in shock. She had the cheek to ask him about **his** mental health when **she** was the one who was talking gibberish? He lowered himself in his usual chair. 'Take your time.'

'Don't worry, I will.'

'Good.' Walter had to have a last word. He didn't know why, he just had to.

Listening to her car door slam and Beth gunning the engine, he let out a sigh. So far, this day was an unmitigated disaster. Goodness knows how bad the rest of them would be whilst she was under his roof.

'Nasty, horrible, vile, obnoxious,' Beth muttered under her breath as she tore off down the lane. 'Pig-headed, crabby, bloody-minded...' she added, braking as she rounded the corner, to reach the junction at the bottom of Muddypuddle Lane at a more reasonable speed.

Feeling a sudden urge to see if they'd started work on her house (this was only day three of Hot Water Tank Horror, but she hoped they would have done **something**) she parked outside and got out.

The house was as quiet as the grave and when she peered through the window, her hands cupped around the glass, she was dismayed to see that the living room looked exactly as she had last seen it. Not a single piece of plasterboard had been removed.

Beth felt like crying. But instead of having a weep, she drew on her infuriation with Walter and strode off in the direction of the high street.

'I'm here about my house,' she announced as soon as she stepped inside, ignoring a youngish couple who were sitting at the desk and talking to Zander.

He had frozen in the middle of a sentence, his eyes darting from her face to the office door and back again as he muttered, 'Oh, god.'

'No, just Mrs Fairfax. What are you doing about my house?'

'Um…'

'I've just come from there, and nothing's been done. Not. A. Thing.'

'We're, um, awaiting instructions from the landlord.'

'What's his phone number? I'll give him a ring myself.'

'I'm sorry, Mrs Fairfax, but we're acting as the letting agent so everything needs to be done through us.'

'But that's the problem – nothing **is** being done. I want to know when I can move in. Do you realise the conditions I'm living in at the moment?'

 Zander bit his lip. The couple looked like rabbits caught in headlights. Their eyes were out on stalks and they were staring at her as though she'd lost her mind.

Perhaps she had. Walter had the ability to bring out the worst in her.

'Disgraceful, that's what it is,' she cried. 'I can't take much more of it.'

Zander said, 'I'll, um, get onto them right now. In a minute. When I've finished dealing with my current clients.'

'Your **current client** is standing right here and wants you to phone my landlord immediately. I'm not leaving until you do.'

'Go ahead,' the chap said to Zander. 'I think this lady's need is greater than ours.'

Zander nodded, his jaw tense. Beth felt a twinge of remorse, but it didn't last. The chap was right, her need **was** greater.

But Beth wasn't in luck. There was no answer when Zander phoned, and she had to concede defeat. With Zander's promise to keep trying and that he would phone her as soon as he had any news, Beth left his office with a heavy heart.

She really thought she was going to cry, as tears pricked her eyes. Walter was right: she was stupid. She must be, to have thought she could pull this off. She had gone from being comfortable (if somewhat lonely) in her house in Birmingham, to being extremely uncomfortable living in the home of the most obnoxious man on the planet. And she had no one to blame but herself.

Beth felt a touch on her arm as a voice said, 'Hello, Beth. I thought it was you.' Lena was standing in front of her, gazing at her in concern. 'Are you okay?'

Beth shook her head. 'Not really.'

'Is there anything I can do to help?'

'Not unless you can magically repair a collapsed ceiling.'

'Oh, dear. Do you want to talk about it? We could go for a coffee. Things often seem better after a chat.'

Beth didn't think it would be better at all, but a coffee and a chat would be very welcome, nevertheless.

As soon as they were settled in the squishy chairs near the window, cappuccinos in hand, Lena wanted to know what had got Beth so upset.

'It's Walter,' Beth said, and went on to explain.

Lena listened without interruption, until Beth ground to a halt, embarrassed. 'It sounds so daft when I say it out loud,' she muttered. 'He's not a bad person, but he's not the easiest man to get on with, and when the pair of us are together we fight like two rats in a bag.'

Lena said, 'I don't know Walter particularly well, but Amos does. He reckons Walter is a typical farmer: stoic and taciturn, but he's got a heart of gold.'

'He hides it well.'

'I might be wrong, but I think he's had a lot of heartache in his life. His wife died when Otto was a teenager, and Walter raised him whilst trying to keep the farm going. That can't have been easy.'

'No, it can't,' Beth agreed softly. She hadn't realised. She knew all too well how hard it was being a single parent.

'And there was all that trouble before Dulcie took over the farm.'

'What trouble?'

'Don't you know?'

'Dulcie mentioned something about Otto having to raffle the farm off, but I couldn't have been listening.'

Lena studied her. 'What I'm about to tell you is common knowledge, so I'm not speaking out of turn or breaking any confidences, but it might help you understand Walter a bit better. Hang on.' She beckoned the waitress over and ordered two more coffees.

Beth was intrigued. She hadn't really gone into the details of how Dulcie had acquired the farm. All she knew was that her daughter had won it in a lottery and that it used to belong to Walter. Dulcie was forever complaining that the farm was a money pit – hence the drive to make soap, sell goats milk, have open days, and so on – so Beth had assumed that running a sheep farm had got too much for Walter, and he had decided to retire. At around the same time, Otto had come back to Picklewick to live, and the two of them, father and son, had moved into the cottage on Muddypuddle Lane when Dulcie had acquired the farm.

Lena drank some of her coffee and settled back. 'Walter has kept that farm going singlehandedly since Otto left to go to catering college. It's not easy being a farmer, but he was fifteen, maybe twenty years younger then, and he coped. But gradually he stopped coping. Amos feels guilty because he had no idea that Walter was struggling, until the Christmas before last when he collapsed and was rushed into hospital. When Otto came to see him, he realised that not only was Walter mentally and physically exhausted, but he had also run up huge debts trying to keep the farm afloat. Dealing with all that worry, whilst hiding it from everyone – Otto included – had taken its toll, and

Amos told me that Otto had worried that Walter wouldn't recover. I must admit that I was shocked when I saw him; he was all skin and bone, and looked so frail... I didn't recognise him.'

Beth hadn't touched her drink. She was far too caught up in the tale Lena was telling.

Lena continued, 'Amos reckons Walter feels guilty because Otto had to give up his job in London to look after him, even though it has all worked out brilliantly in the end.'

Beth couldn't disagree with that. Dulcie and Otto were perfect for each other, and the move from London hadn't impacted Otto's career. On the contrary, he now had a book deal he wouldn't otherwise have had and owned his own restaurant.

'Walter was devastated, of course,' Lena was saying. 'He'd lived on that farm all his life. It must have been awful to see it raffled off.'

Beth wished she'd known this earlier. It was her own fault for not being more interested, and she felt guilty and ashamed for judging him so harshly. His tale didn't detract from the fact that he was grumpy and argumentative, but she could now understand why – to a certain extent.

Feeling better about returning to the cottage on Muddypuddle Lane and vowing (yet again) to be more sympathetic towards Walter, Beth drank her coffee, glad that Lena had explained. And when the conversation moved away from Walter and onto their respective families and other things, Beth hoped that she had made her first real friend in Picklewick.

CHAPTER SEVEN

Walter hoped that an afternoon of retail therapy would have put Beth in a better mood. He wasn't going to hold his breath, though. He was, however, desperate for a bath.

With Peg at his heels, Walter made his way to the bottom of the stairs and stared up. Feeling stronger than he had felt when he'd attempted the stairs in the farmhouse, and more confident with Beth out of the way, it seemed an ideal opportunity to give them a go. It was going to be a challenge getting up them whilst hanging onto his crutches, but he thought he could do it.

Parking his backside on the second step, he used his good leg and one arm to ease himself onto the next, then repeated the performance. So far, so good. Feeling pleased with himself, he carried on this way until he eventually reached the top. He'd even managed to keep hold of his crutches. Result!

Making sure he was well away from the yawning stairwell, Walter clambered to his feet, using the banister for leverage. It was hard work, and he was hot and out of breath by the time he was fully upright. But the novelty of being upstairs in his own home was worth it, as it meant he could have the bath he so desperately wanted, and he would be able to sleep in his own bed tonight. Ha! That'll show 'em! A couple of days of this, and he would be able to send Beth packing.

Aware that she might return any minute, he gathered some fresh clothes from his bedroom and limped to the bathroom but couldn't resist a quick look in the spare room on his way.

Beth had laid out some things on the chest of drawers, make-up and whatnot, and her case had been placed neatly underneath the window. He refrained from looking inside the wardrobe, guessing that she had probably unpacked. It unnerved him to think that it was **her** clothes hanging in there and not **Otto's**. It gave her presence an air of permanence that her short stay didn't warrant.

Huffing to himself, he locked the bathroom door and lowered his backside onto the closed lid of the toilet, grunting with relief as he took the weight off his good leg. When he'd got his breath back, Walter turned on the hot water tap in the bath, steam gradually filling the room as he undressed.

It wasn't easy trying to ease the jogging bottoms that Otto had lent him over the plaster cast, but he finally managed it. Thankful that when Otto had renovated the cottage, he'd had the foresight to put in a bath with handles (futureproofing, his son had called it), Walter sat on the edge. Then putting his good leg in the bath and keeping his broken one raised and stuck out at an awkward angle so it didn't get wet, he eased himself down into the water.

The splash when his behind hit the bottom of the bath made him wince as a mini tsunami slopped over the side, but the watery mess was immediately forgotten as the lower half of his body was immersed in lovely hot water. It was a bit uncomfortable with one leg stuck over the side, but Walter didn't mind, as he happily soaped himself. This was so much better than trying to stand in the shower (Otto never did manage to find anything for him to sit on) and he even began to hum a little tune.

However, the humming stopped when, some time later and after several attempts, he realised he couldn't get out. Walter was well and truly stuck. Bugger!

He sat there for a while, topping up the hot water when it started to cool and straining to listen to any sounds from downstairs.

When he finally heard the front door open and close he breathed a sigh of relief: rescue was at hand.

'Walter?' Beth called.

'Up here!' He heard her tread on the stairs and recognised the creak on the landing as she reached the top.

'I see you managed the stairs,' she said.

He heard her walk into the spare room, and the sound of the wardrobe door opening.

'Beth?'

'What?'

God, he hated this. 'I'm stuck.'

'Stuck?' Footsteps hurried into his bedroom and hurried back out again. 'Are you in the bathroom?'

'Yes.'

'What do you mean stuck? Please don't tell me you can't get off the toilet.'

'I can't get out of the bath.' He thought he heard a snort of laughter but he couldn't be certain. 'You can't come in,' he added.

'How do you suggest I get you out, if I can't come in?' She tried the handle. The door didn't budge. 'Did you lock it?'

'Yes.'

'Oh, Walter. What were you thinking?'

That he hadn't wanted the worry of her walking in on him whilst he was naked in the tub – that was what he had been thinking. Now though, he would be perfectly happy for her to see him in the altogether if it meant he could get out of this blasted bath.

'Are you any good at picking locks?' he asked.

'Yeah, I'm an expert. I'll just go get my hat pin.'

'No need to be sarcastic.'

'I might be able to break the door down,' she called.

 Walter rolled his eyes. 'You're almost seventy; you'll break your shoulder, not the door.'

'I won't if I use a sledgehammer. I bet Dulcie's got one.'

Walter baulked. 'You're **not** using a sledgehammer on my door.'

 'How else do you suggest I get you out?' Her tone became sly. 'Perhaps I should phone Otto.'

'Don't you dare!' If Otto knew about this, Walter would end up back at the farmhouse faster than Peg gobbled her dinner.

He thought frantically. They had to do something. He couldn't stay here for much longer – he was starting to look even more prune-like than he was already.

The lock was an old-fashioned one with a key, because both Walter and Otto had wanted to keep as many of the cottage's period features as possible. Apart from the kitchen. Otto had insisted on installing a state-of-the-art kitchen, and Walter didn't have the heart to refuse him. His son had sacrificed so much already…

Walter didn't know if his idea would work, but he wanted to give it a shot. 'Can you go out to the shed?' he called. 'Find a thin screwdriver and bring my newspaper up.'

To be fair to Beth, she didn't waste time asking why. He listened to her trot downstairs and waited impatiently for her to return.

'Got 'em,' she announced. 'Now what?'

'Slide the newspaper under the door, then see if you can poke the screwdriver into the lock and wiggle it until the key falls out.'

 'Nice.' She sounded impressed and Walter puffed out his chest.

It was far too soon to give himself a pat on the back though, because his idea mightn't work. He had seen it done in a film once, but what happened on screen probably wouldn't work in real life.

Walter held his breath as he heard scraping noises coming from the direction of the lock, then he let it out in a whoosh as he saw the key begin to wiggle.

'Newspaper!' he yelled, realising that she had forgotten it, and his heart was in his mouth until Beth had shoved it underneath the door.

He hadn't realised until now just how much of a gap there was between the door and the lino; no wonder he could feel a draft when he sat on the loo. It was something that needed to be fixed, but right now he was extremely grateful for it.

His attention was firmly on the door, as the barrel of the key was slowly pushed out of the lock. It hung there for a moment, and once again he held his breath. When it finally dropped directly onto the newspaper, Walter let out a whoop and slapped the water, sending it sloshing over the side.

'The key is out!' he cried. 'Pull the newspaper towards you.' Then he abruptly deflated with the fear that it mightn't fit under the door, especially with there being carpet on the other side.

He couldn't look. Screwing his eyes shut, Walter ground his teeth, praying that Beth would be able to retrieve the key.

When he heard it turn in the lock and the door click open, he could have wept for joy. Until he remembered he was starkers. His eyes flew open and he grabbed a towel off the rail to cover his embarrassment.

Beth was standing in the doorway. He fully expected her to smirk, but she wore an odd expression, one that he couldn't decode.

Walter flushed under her gaze, even though his modesty was preserved by the towel. 'Good job,' he said.

Seeming to snap out of whatever had got hold of her, Beth snatched up another towel and stepped towards him. He appreciated that she kept her eyes averted, as she held out a hand. Grasping it, Walter got his good leg into what he hoped was the correct position to bear his weight.

'One, two, three,' Beth chanted, and on 'three' she leant back and heaved.

Walter emerged from the bath like Neptune rising from the waves, only with considerably less grandeur. Water cascaded over the floor, but he was upright and that was all he was concerned about.

Feeling more foolish than he had ever felt in his life, he perched his scrawny backside on the edge of the bath and swung his legs to the floor. Beth, he noticed, had her head turned away and was steadfastly gazing at the ceiling.

Without looking at him, she handed him the dry towel. 'Can you take it from here, or do you need me to help you get dressed?'

'I can manage.' His voice was hoarse. 'Thanks'

A smile teased the corners of her mouth. She looked so much nicer when she smiled. She should do it more often, he thought.

She said, 'You're welcome. I'll be downstairs. Shout when you need me.'

When. Not **if**. It seemed that Beth was just as aware as Walter that he needed far more help than he cared to admit.

The last thing Beth had expected to see when she returned to the cottage was a naked man stuck in a bath. She had to admit that she had felt acutely embarrassed, but probably not as embarrassed as Walter! His face had been a picture, she thought, as she basted the pork chops she was cooking for their tea. But his face was the only thing she had looked at. The rest of him had been strictly out of bounds.

However, she had caught a glimpse of his chest and the smattering of grizzled grey hairs covering it. The sight had given her a bit of a pang. It was a long time – many years – since she had been within touching distance of a bare male chest

She had quickly looked away. Such pangs belonged in her past, when she had been young enough to have done something about them. These days she didn't have the energy nor the inclination.

Companionship wouldn't go amiss though. That was what she had missed when the kids were growing up: someone to share her worries with at the end of a difficult day, or to share the joys when good things happened. She even missed washing up whilst someone else dried. Not that her husband (God rest his soul) had wielded a tea towel very often. Or listened when she needed a good grizzle. He'd not been there for many of the good times either, now that she came to think of it. So what was it exactly, that she missed? How could you miss something that you'd never had?

Beth shook her head to clear it of such fanciful thoughts. It wasn't surprising that she was out-of-sorts, considering the stressful few days she'd had. And there were likely to be more stressful days to come.

Beth suppressed a snort: her day hadn't been half as stressful as Walter's. He'd had a right old time of it. At one point she had honestly feared she wasn't going to be able to get the door open by herself – unless she used the sledgehammer.

But try explaining a smashed door to Otto. He was bound to notice, although maybe they could have kept it from him long enough to convince him that Walter didn't need looking after. Beth hadn't wanted to take the risk though, and neither had Walter. He wanted her gone almost as much as she wanted to leave. Although he might change his mind when she plonked a nice pork chop with roast potatoes and veg in front of him. She bet he wouldn't manage to cook a meal like that whilst balancing on one leg!

The evening meal wasn't as uncomfortable as lunch had been, despite the events of earlier, and Beth began to relax.

When Walter asked, 'Did you get what you needed in the village?' she didn't go looking for a hidden meaning or disguised sarcasm, and took the question at face value.

'Yes and no. I called into the estate agent because I checked on the house and noticed they hadn't started on the repairs. I didn't get much joy.' She spooned out a portion of apple sauce and popped it on her plate, before offering the bowl to Walter.

He tasted the sauce and his eyes widened. 'Did you make this yourself?'

'I did. And the stuffing and the Yorkshire puds.'

'Very tasty.' Beth inclined her head in acknowledgement.

She had always been a dab hand in the kitchen, and it was a pleasure to see someone enjoy her cooking again. These past couple of years, Maisie, although still living at home until recently, had been out more often than she'd been in, and Beth had stopped cooking tea for her because she'd hated wasting food. This meal definitely wasn't going to waste, she was pleased to see, as Walter tucked in with enthusiasm.

'That's the no bit,' he said. 'What's the yes?'

'You're eating it. I also bumped into Lena, and we had a coffee.'

'Lovely woman, Lena. Amos has got a good 'un there. Mind you, she hasn't done too badly herself; Amos is the salt of the earth. He'd do anything for you, would Amos. Gotta take it easy though – angina. We're a couple of old crocs. Although at the moment I'd say I'm more croc than he is.' He gestured to his broken leg with his fork. 'Just you wait until I get this cast off – I'll give him a run for his money. Talking about casts, I've got an appointment at the fracture clinic the day after tomorrow. Can you... Do you think...?'

'Yes, I'll drive you there.'

'Thank you.'

Beth wondered if it had hurt him to ask. She knew how much he hated being reliant on her, but Dulcie and Otto were busy; she wasn't. It felt rather good to be needed again, even if it was Walter who was the one needing it.

Surprisingly, he hadn't needed help getting dressed after his bath, and neither had he needed her assistance in getting down the stairs. He'd inched down on his bottom, although Beth had held his crutches. It would be handy if he had a pair for upstairs use, she'd mused, and she'd made a mental note to ask Lena if she knew where she could get hold of a spare pair.

After Beth had stacked the dishwasher (she'd never had one of those and had needed to pick Walter's brains on how to work it, the same as she'd had to ask him about the stove), the two of them settled down in front of the telly with a cup of tea and a custard cream or two.

Despite being on her own with Walter and not having Dulcie or Otto as a buffer, Beth felt more relaxed in the cottage than she had in the farmhouse. Probably because Walter wasn't being so tetchy, she surmised. By unspoken mutual agreement neither of them had mentioned the bathroom incident when Dulcie had phoned to check that they hadn't killed each other yet, nor when Otto had popped in on his way to the restaurant to see how they were getting on (i.e. no fatalities) and ask whether they needed anything.

Having a secret seemed to have broken a barrier between them, and even though Beth didn't want to be here and Walter didn't want her here, there appeared to be a ceasefire for the moment. How long it would last was anyone's guess, but Beth wasn't going to look a gift horse in the mouth.

As she got ready for her first night under Walter's roof, she wondered how much her new-found reluctance to wind him up was due to what Lena had told her, and she could feel herself softening towards him.

If this evening was anything to go by, maybe looking after him for a few days wouldn't be such a strain after all.

Walter didn't know what the technical word was for the gadget that enabled him to pick things up off the floor (he called it the 'grabby thing'), but it didn't half come in handy this morning to retrieve his dropped sock.

He was currently sitting on his bed, getting dressed for his hospital appointment and feeling rather nervous. He hoped everything was okay under the cast.

Eventually dressed (everything took three times as long with a broken leg, he had discovered), he lowered himself cautiously down the stairs and limped into the kitchen. The delicious aroma of bacon had made his tummy rumble in anticipation whilst he was upstairs, and he was eager to tuck into his breakfast.

Beth was standing by the stove, wielding a frying pan. 'Pancakes, and bacon with syrup for breakfast,' she announced. 'Go sit down, it's almost ready.'

She joined him at the table, her own plate piled just as high as his, and he reckoned that both of them needed to keep their strength up for the ordeal ahead. Him, because he hated hospitals and wasn't relishing having his leg poked and prodded, and Beth because she had confessed to him that she was fearful of driving on strange roads.

Her admission had surprised him: he'd been under the impression that nothing fazed her. Over the past couple of days, since **Bathgate**, he had begun to notice chinks in her armour. Beth Fairfax wasn't as indomitable as she appeared. She was still grouchy though, and they'd had a couple of spats, but nothing like it had been.

Walter was quietly hopeful that things were settling down.

He was also quietly hopeful that he might have his house to himself again shortly. Maybe this hospital visit would help move things on. If he had a good report from the fracture clinic, it might give him more leverage in persuading Otto that he could manage without Beth's help.

Although, Walter had to admit, having Beth around did make life easier. She cooked a mean breakfast, for one, and she took Peg out for her daily constitutional for another. Maybe he should keep her around for a while longer.

He was still mulling it over on the drive to Thornbury and the hospital, and he continued to think about it after the doctor had announced that she was pleased with his progress and would see him again in four weeks.

Realistically, he knew that he still needed help with many things and having Beth here was the easiest option. Besides, he was getting rather used to her.

'Do you fancy stopping off somewhere for a spot of lunch?' Beth asked, as she drove out of the hospital's congested car park.

'What about my leg?'

'You can bring it with you,' she replied, deadpan.

Walter rolled his eyes. 'I meant, should I be out and about with it?'

'I don't see why not. It's not as though you're ill, or contagious. You see people with broken legs all the time.'

Walter didn't like to admit that he was worried someone might bump it, or that he wouldn't be able to make it from the car to wherever it was they were going. It had been difficult enough walking from the patient drop-off area to the fracture clinic's waiting room.

'Breakfast filled me up,' he said by way of an excuse, even though he didn't want to go home just yet. He was quite enjoying being out of the house.

Beth was staring straight ahead, her attention on the road as she negotiated the traffic through the busy town. But Walter could have sworn that there was a disappointed set to her shoulders.

Relenting, he said, 'There's a pub called The Dancing Pheasant halfway between here and Picklewick. It used to have a good reputation, but I don't know what it's like now. We could give it a go, if you want.' Then he decided to be honest with her; after all, she had shared her concern about driving on unfamiliar roads with him. 'I'm worried about knocking my leg, or not being able to walk far,' he confessed. 'The pub has got its own car park.'

Beth shot him a glance before hurriedly looking at the road again. 'Sorry, Walter, I didn't think.'

Wow! Beth had apologised?! That didn't happen very often.

'I'm surprised I'm hungry at all after bacon and pancakes,' he said. 'But I am.'

'Me, too. Shall we give it a go?'

So they did. And very pleasant it was.

To Walter's surprise they had quite a lot to chat about, and he found himself enjoying her company. Lunch was bitter-sweet though, because the last time he'd been out for a meal with a woman it had been with his wife, when she was alive. Not that they'd gone out for meals much: that had been reserved for special occasions.

Still, this was very nice and as they waited for dessert and coffee, he sat back with a contented sigh.

'This is a real treat,' Beth said. 'I don't eat out very often – unless you call having a cuppa in a cafe and smuggling in a packet of Fig Rolls, eating out.'

'I don't eat out at all,' Walter said. 'Except for going to Dulcie's.'

'What about the pub? Do you ever go to the Black Horse?'

'Now and again, but not for a meal. I used to play darts.' He hadn't played for a long time. Now that he came to think about it there were lots of things he hadn't done for a long time, and he realised how insular he had become over the years.

'Is there much to do in Picklewick?' Beth asked.

Walter's mind went blank. 'I've no idea.'

'I wondered what was on at the community centre.' She got out her phone, the tip of her tongue poking out as she scrolled, and Walter could imagine her doing the same thing in school when she was a girl, as she worked on her sums or concentrated on her spellings. The image made him smile.

'Yoga, mother and toddler group, photography club, bingo, knit and natter... And The Black Horse has a quiz night and karaoke. Can you sing?' she asked.

'Er, no.'

'Me, neither. I sound like a scalded cat. Knit?'

Walter shook his head.

'Do you like quizzes?'

'I don't mind Tipping Point on TV, and I quite like The Chase.'

'Wanna give it a go?'

'Oh, I don't think so. I can't see myself being on TV, can you?'

Beth chortled. 'Not on the telly! Down the pub.'

Walter blinked. 'Maybe.'

Beth carried on, 'There's a gardening club.' She wrinkled her nose. 'Nah, if I feel the urge to get my hands dirty, I'll ask Dulcie if I can grub about in her veggie patch.' Beth fell silent for a moment, her eyes on the screen, then she yelled, 'Kite flying!' and Walter almost leapt out of his skin.

'Where?' His gaze shot to the window.

'There's a kite flying club,' Beth explained. 'I quite fancy flying a kite again. I haven't done that since I was a kid. Pendine Sands in West Wales. We had a caravan for a week.' She looked wistful.

Their desserts arrived, along with their coffee, but Beth didn't begin to eat hers straight away; she was busily typing one-fingered into her phone.

Walter was tempted to tell her off, the way he'd heard her reprimand Maisie for playing with her phone at the table, but he held his tongue.

Then he wished he hadn't when Beth made an announcement. 'Righty-ho, I've just signed us up for Half Board on Thursday afternoon.' And when Walter stared at her in confusion, she explained, 'It's an afternoon of board games. And on the following Monday we're going to bingo.'

'I don't like bingo.'

'Have you ever been?'

'No, but—'

'Don't knock it until you try it,' she said, around a mouthful of apple crumble and custard. 'If you give it a go and still don't like it, we can try something else.'

'What if I don't want to?'

'I'll go on my own, and you can be Mr Boring all by yourself.'

'I'm not boring,' he protested.

'Prove it!'

Walter pulled a face. He didn't think he could. In fact, he was fairly certain that he **was** boring. Maybe playing board games and so on was the sort of thing that might help alleviate the loneliness he had been feeling...

It looked like he would be going to bingo after all!

CHAPTER EIGHT

Beth had never seen a cribbage board before, and she gazed at it with a mixture of puzzlement and disbelief. The block of wood was about a foot long and had a succession of tiny holes drilled into it, running along its length in two parallel rows of two. Four small brass pegs had been set in the board.

Walter moved all the pegs to the one end of the board, saying, 'The winner is the first to reach 121 points.'

Beth didn't have a clue how points were gained, and she was even more bemused when Walter produced a pack of cards and began to explain the rules.

They sounded rather complicated.

When Beth had booked them into Half Board (so called, she found out, because the session was only ever half a day) she had imagined Scrabble, or Monopoly. But Walter's eyes had lit up when he had spied the crib board, and she didn't have the heart to refuse him when he'd suggested a game.

He even seemed enthusiastic about teaching her to play, although she suspected he might change his mind when he realised that the rules were going over her head. Blankly she stared at the hand he'd dealt her, wondering what she was supposed to do with it. His explanation of her having to decide which two cards to discard, had passed her by.

'Walter?' someone said, and Beth glanced up to see a dapper chap in his seventies, with salt-and-pepper hair and a moustache beaming down at them.

'Remember me? Stanley Childs?' the old fella asked, holding out his hand. Walter began to struggle to his feet, but the man gently pushed him back down. 'Don't get up,' Stanley said. 'I heard you'd broken your leg.' He turned his attention to Beth. 'Aren't you going to introduce me to your lady friend?'

Beth snorted. Lady friend, indeed. And she didn't need 'introducing'; she was perfectly capable of introducing herself.

'Beth Fairfax,' she said, before Walter could open his mouth.

Stanley shook her hand, holding onto it for longer than was strictly necessary. His gaze locked onto hers. 'Charmed,' he said. 'Fairfax… Now where have I…? Oh, yes! Otto's better half, Dulcie. You must be her sister.'

Beth rolled her eyes and giggled, despite herself. Walter shot her a cross look.

Stanley didn't appear to notice. 'How long are you in Picklewick?' Stanley asked.

'Permanently,' Beth replied.

'Are you living at the farm?'

'No, she's living with me,' Walter interjected.

'I see.' Stanley's eyebrows shot up.

'It's a temporary arrangement,' Beth leapt in before Stanley got the wrong end of the stick. She didn't want him to think that she and Walter were an item, not when Stanley was so handsome and suave. She wasn't too keen on his moustache, which was a bit too handlebar-ish for her liking, but the rest of him was easy on the eye, and she bet he was a hit with Picklewick's female contingent – the older ones, that is. Such as herself.

She was so glad she hadn't had to twist Walter's arm to persuade him to come with her today. If she'd had to come on her own, she probably wouldn't have bothered. Or rather, she wouldn't have had the courage. Walking into a roomful of strangers terrified her, especially when they undoubtedly knew each other. She would have felt like the new girl in school, and probably would have turned tail and run. Now, though, she knew Stanley, so if she did come on her own next time, she mightn't be quite as nervous.

'I'll leave you to it,' Stanley was saying.

Beth didn't want him to go. And the reason was that she really didn't want to learn how to play cribbage – or any other card game, for that matter. She had her eye on a group of ladies who were setting up a game of Cluedo, which was more to her liking.

She said to Stanley, 'Do you know how to play cribbage?'

'I do. Why, would you like to challenge me to a game? I warn you, I like to win.'

'Good. So does Walter.' She got to her feet. 'Take my place. I'm sure Walter would prefer to play against someone who knows what they're doing.'

Stanley looked startled. 'Three can play crib, you know.'

Beth sent Walter an apologetic smile. 'I haven't played board games for ages. Let me ease myself in slowly with a nice game of Cluedo – if those ladies will have me – and I promise I'll give cribbage a go next time.'

And with that, she shot off, feeling Walter and Stanley's gaze following her.

But when she neared the table where the ladies were about to begin their game, her courage failed her and she swerved off in the direction of the loos that she'd noticed on the way into the community centre (at her age it was always wise to know where the nearest toilet was), and she hurriedly inside.

When she emerged, the first thing she noticed was that Walter was sitting on his own. The second was that the cribbage board had disappeared and in its place was another game. **Cluedo.**

'Stanley's gone to fetch us some tea,' Walter said. 'When he comes back, how about a nice game of Cluedo?'

Beth could have kissed him.

Bingo. Ugh. Walter surveyed the community hall with suspicion. Roughly fifteen tables were laid out with four or so chairs at each. At the far end of the room, on the stage, was another table with a round black basket containing a number of white balls, and a microphone. Behind it, and off to the side, was a second table displaying a variety of objects. It reminded him of a raffle table.

Walter had never played bingo in his life and, seeing the avaricious faces of the people gathered there, he wasn't sure he wanted to start now.

'Ooh, you can win a fish and chip supper, or a bottle of sherry,' Beth said, spying the table of prizes. 'I'm partial to a glass of sherry.' She smacked her lips.

Walter preferred beer, or whisky, if he was forced to choose something stronger.

Lowering himself into a chair, he studied the bingo card.

What he didn't like about bingo was the element of luck. There appeared to be no skill involved whatsoever, but remembering Beth telling him not to knock it until he tried it, he decided to keep an open mind. After all, he had enjoyed playing Cluedo the other day – although, he hadn't enjoyed Stanley being part of the game. Stanley was too suave for

Walter's liking. Or would **smarmy** be a better description?

Stanley thought he was the bee's knees. He had always been the same. Walter remembered him from school, and the girls had fallen over him then. The man had had two wives, one deceased and one divorced, and Walter suspected he was on the lookout for number three. Walter hoped Stanley hadn't set his sights on Beth. She was too good for the likes of Stanley Childs.

As the thought went through Walter's head, he was pulled up short.

A week ago, he would have been happy for Stanley to go gunning after Beth. He probably would have thought they deserved each other.

But not now. When it came to Beth, Walter had undergone a seismic shift. And it had taken another man's interest in her to make him realise that he actually liked her. **Liked** not **tolerated**.

Well, well, well... That was a turn-up for the books, he thought. In fact, he felt quite proprietorial over her, and he didn't want to see her get hurt. Stanley was a user, a player, a ladies' man. Beth deserved better.

Beth heard the sound of the shower going and she smiled. The little plastic stool she had found in the charity shop in the village had been perfect for Walter to sit in in the cubicle. It was a bit on the low side, but she'd made him practice getting up from it before he'd given it a go in the shower. He still needed help waterproofing his cast though, because he couldn't quite reach to put a plastic bag over it. Unlike Beth, who was quite flexible for her age, Walter was as stiff as a board.

However, Beth had a plan to do something about that, and as soon as he was dressed and downstairs, she would put that plan into action.

They were going to Dulcie's for Sunday lunch (Beth was looking forward to seeing everyone), but they had a couple of hours before they needed to leave and she intended to use the time wisely.

'Armchair yoga,' she announced, when Walter appeared in the living room.

'Is this another one of your hare-brained activities?' Walter was smiling, so she didn't take offence.

'This one is for your benefit, not mine,' she retorted. 'I'm bendy enough. See?' She bent over, touching the carpet with her fingers. There was a time when she used to be able to put her palms flat on the floor, but that had been before she'd had the kids. Nowadays, her tummy got in the way and her boobs threatened to unbalance her.

When she straightened up, Walter's eyes were on stalks. 'Please tell me you're not expecting me to touch my toes,' he begged.

'Not straight away, but eventually you should be able to. And when your cast is off, you'll find it much easier to bend and stretch.'

Walter stared at her, and she realised she wouldn't be living here when the cast was removed. That's what they were working towards, wasn't it – him managing on his own and her moving back in with Dulcie (or into her own house, if the repairs were completed). But, oddly enough, that goal no longer seemed as imperative as it had when she had agreed to move into the cottage on Muddypuddle Lane.

Aside from those first few days when she had wished she was anywhere but here,

Beth had settled into life in Walter's house surprisingly well. She thought they muddled along together quite nicely now. They still bickered a bit, but nowhere near as badly as they used to. She would miss the place when she left. Without her realising it, the cottage had gradually come to feel like home. But what was even more surprising (disturbing, actually) was that she would miss Walter. Unbeknownst to him, he had provided the company she craved and, on occasion, she felt as though they were an old married couple – without the obvious; they didn't share a bedroom.

As Beth watched Walter expertly manoeuvre himself into his seat, something about that last thought niggled at her, but she couldn't put her finger on it.

Then she let out a gasp as it came to her: her and Walter **in the same bed.**

 A flush spread up her chest into her neck and her face, and she felt a flutter in her tummy.

'Did you sprain something?' Walter asked. 'All that bending and stretching is bound to put your back out.'

'I'm fine,' she retorted. 'Hot flush.' Beth fanned herself vigorously with her hands, flapping them in front of her face and hoping that any mention of the menopause would have him changing the subject rapidly. She also hoped that he didn't realise she was too old for a hot flush. She was thankfully past all that, although she had heard of some poor women who continued to have them into their seventies.

True enough, Walter looked petrified at the thought that she might feel tempted to expand further and he seemed more than happy when she returned to the subject of armchair yoga.

'Sit up straight,' she commanded. 'Hands on your knees. Close your eyes and breathe.'

'I always breathe.'

Beth sat down in the adjacent chair, her back ramrod straight. 'You need to do it mindfully,' she said, remembering the online tutorial she had watched earlier.

'How do you mean **mindfully**?'

'Breathe from the stomach and think about it as you're doing it. In through the nose, hold it for a second, then out through the mouth.'

'It's a load of old cod's wallop, if you ask me. People have been breathing for thousands of years and they didn't need anyone to tell them how to do it.' He opened one eye and squinted at her.

Beth glared at him. With a resigned shake of his head, he closed it again.

Beth watched him carefully, telling herself that it was to make sure he didn't cheat, but in reality she was enjoying gazing at him. He was relaxed, the lines in his face not as prominent, and he looked considerably better than the day Dulcie and Otto had brought him home from hospital, and although Beth couldn't take all the credit, she took some. Hearty, regular meals, someone to do his laundry and cleaning, someone to make sure he was okay... It made a difference.

'Can I stop breathing now?' he asked.

'Better not,' Beth chortled. 'You'll keel over.'

'You know what I mean.'

'You can open your eyes,' she conceded. 'We're going to do thoracic rotations next.'

'Eh?'

'Put your hands behind your head, like when you were in school, then twist to face that way—' She twisted her head and torso to the left. 'Then this way.' She twisted to the right. 'We do this ten times each side. One, two...'

Walter copied her, but they were twisting in opposite directions, so with every second twist they found themselves staring each other in the eye. Beth was glad when they'd finished that exercise.

'Are we done?' he asked.

'No. Next, we drop our heads to our chests.' She demonstrated. Walter followed suit. 'Can you feel the stretch in your neck?'

'I can feel something. I think I've done myself a mischief.'

Beth ignored his grumbling. 'Sit up and look straight ahead, arching your back slightly. And repeat,' she sang.

Ten of those and she was starting to feel a little dizzy from all the bending and stretching. Determined to plough on and convinced that it was doing them some good (it might take a while for the benefits to become apparent), Beth showed him how to flop forwards so that his head was between his knees.

It was called the rag doll position, but Walter looked more like a broken doll by the time he had attempted ten of those. Beth wasn't feeling much better. She thought of herself as fairly fit for her age (there was that phrase again, **for her age**) but clearly she wasn't, because the deep breathing she had been trying to do had become more of a pant and a grunt.

Poor Walter's face was slowly turning purple with the effort. 'This is supposed to be good for you?' he puffed as he straightened up.

'Shall we do some arm exercises now?'

'Goodie. I can't wait.'

Beth rolled her eyes and tried not to tut. The ungrateful so-and-so. However, she had to admit that it was harder work than the man in the video had led her to believe.

After windmilling their arms around and trying (unsuccessfully) to grab their hands behind their backs, Beth called it a day.

'The rest of them involve standing next to your chair,' she explained, 'but I don't think you're up for that.' A giggle escaped her. 'There is one exercise you've already mastered though...'

'What's that?' Walter winced as he rubbed his shoulder.

'Standing on one leg,' she laughed. 'It's called **the stork**, but you're supposed to alternate which leg you stand on.'

'Very funny.' He didn't appear amused.

'We'll have another go tomorrow,' she promised. 'Ten minutes every day and you'll be a new man.'

'I'm quite partial to the old one,' he said.

Funnily enough, so was Beth...

Painting and drawing weren't Walter's forte. He hardly knew one end of a pencil from another, and the only time he had held a paintbrush was when he'd been nagged into redecorating. But here was Beth, insisting that they give an art class a go.

She said, 'You enjoyed Half Board.'

They'd been twice now, and Walter did enjoy it, especially since Stanley hadn't shown his face last time. 'I didn't like bingo,' he argued.

'But at least you tried it. And you won a powder puff and mirror set.'

'You may have noticed that I didn't bring it home with me.'

'You could have regifted it.'

'I think it had been regifted too many times already.'

'You're probably right.'

Walter glared at her suspiciously. He wasn't often right, and he wondered whether she was being sarcastic.

Once again, they headed for the heart of the village and the community centre. Walter was quietly impressed at how much went on inside the unassuming red-brick building. It was nothing to look at on the outside, being shabby and unappealing, but inside was an Aladdin's cave of clubs and activities, this morning's being an art class.

Walter wasn't surprised to see some familiar faces as many of the same people tended to frequent the same clubs and classes. It seemed that the village had an active troop of enthusiastic pensioners, and it looked like he was going to be one of them if Beth had her way.

Several easels had been placed in a circle, around something that Walter could only describe as a chaise longue. He eyed it doubtfully, hoping he wasn't expected to draw it, because it wasn't particularly inspiring. He had been expecting a bowl of fruit, if he was honest. It was a nice shade of red though, so maybe the class was doing the colour red this week...? He wasn't sure how these things worked.

 A plump woman wearing a multi-coloured kaftan and lots of chunky jewellery spotted him and Beth hovering in the doorway, and she hurried forward.

'Hello, hello, come on in, we don't bite – not unless we're drawing teeth, ha, ha! Welcome to Art for Art's Sake. I'm Melanie, your teacher. Have you done much drawing or painting? Never mind if you haven't – everyone has to start somewhere, and we're a non-judgemental lot. Would you like to sit next to each other? Of course you would. What's your name?'

'Walter,' he mumbled, wondering when the woman was going to draw breath.

'Walter, you can sit here, and—?'

'Beth,' Beth supplied.

'You can sit here. Did you bring an overall or a pinny? No? Not a problem, I've always got spares.' She pointed to a box in the corner. 'We'll be working with pencil or charcoal today, whichever you prefer. The paper is already on your easel and so are the pencils. Any questions?'

Walter had one. 'Are they red?'

Melanie blinked. 'Er, no, they're HB pencils. We're not using coloured pencils today. Enjoy the session and shout out if you need any help. I'll be doing the rounds anyway, to see how you're getting on.'

'I thought they'd be red,' he muttered as he hobbled to his chair, thankful that he wasn't expected to stand. He'd had visions of people pacing around in front of their easels and using the ends of their brushes to check angles and whatnot.

Beth hung her handbag over the back of her chair. 'Why red?'

'That chaise longue thing is red.' He pursed his lips and lowered his voice. 'It's not very interesting, is it? I don't know anything about drawing, but even I can see that with a couple of lines and a squiggle, it'll be done. How long did you say the class was?'

'Two hours, with half an hour in the middle for refreshments.'

'I reckon it'll take me about ten minutes,' he murmured, eyeing up the other artists.

There were about fifteen in all, and the low buzz of conversation filled the air. When Melanie clapped her hands and called for quiet, the room fell silent, the chatter replaced by excited expectation – although what was exciting about a wannabe settee, Walter couldn't imagine.

Melanie said, 'I told you I would have a treat for you, and I know speculation has been rife.' She smiled widely. 'I think many of you have guessed what we're going to be drawing today, so before I bring our model in, I just want to say please don't be embarrassed. The naked human form is the most natural and beautiful thing there is, no matter the age, the shape, or the gender. My advice is to forget that you're drawing a person and concentrate on capturing the essence and the form. Are we ready?'

A chorus of agreement filled the room, but Walter didn't join in. He was starting to get a bad feeling about this.

His fears were confirmed when Melanie opened a door, and cried, 'Artists, here is your model for today – Stanley!'

Walter's horror when Stanley Childs strode into the room, was only exceeded when Stanley removed his robe with a flourish and stood before them with a big grin on his face.

Stanley was naked.

Beth wasn't normally a blusher but when she had caught sight of Stanley in all his proud nakedness, she had felt a whoosh of heat flooding her cheeks. Maybe if she had been more prepared, she wouldn't have reacted as strongly. Walter had let out a gasp along with the other artists, but whilst there had been a flutter of giggles from the rest, he had scowled.

Afterwards, the two of them had immediately fled to The Black Horse for a restorative pint.

Despite having downed half of his ale, Walter looked haunted. Beth might have felt the same if she had spent two hours staring at Stanley's spread-eagled figure, legs akimbo, giving Walter a first-class view of the man's tackle.

'Brazen,' Walter muttered, reaching for his pint and taking a gulp.

Thankfully, Beth's easel had given her a slightly less graphic view, although she had a feeling she might think twice about buying sausages again. Beth suspected that even Melanie, who was probably more used to seeing random naked strangers, had been taken aback by the glee with which Stanley displayed himself. She'd also had a bit of a to-do trying to persuade him to cover up during the interval. It had been enough to put Beth off the Ginger Nuts (an unfortunate choice of biscuit, under the circumstances) although she did rally enough to manage a plain digestive.

'No more art classes,' Walter declared. He had a wild look about his eyes, and Beth could swear his hand was shaking.

'I thought your drawing was rather good.' He shot her a disbelieving look, so she added, 'You captured his expression perfectly. Melanie said it was an interesting caricature.'

Walter had drawn a disembodied head, with an exaggerated Cheshire cat smile and jug ears. Despite it being cartoon-like, it was clearly recognisable as Stanley. Stanley hadn't been amused when he'd seen it, despite Melanie advising him not to look at any of the drawings, and Walter had been on the receiving end of a venomous look.

Stanley hadn't been too enamoured of Beth's attempt either. Despite being able to see Stanley's proudest assets (although she had thought his pride somewhat misplaced), Beth had given him an Action Man anatomy where it counted.

'I need another,' Walter said, draining his glass.

'I think I'll join you.'

'You're driving,' he pointed out.

'We'll get a taxi.'

Drinking brandy this early in the day (it was not quite six o'clock) soon began to take its toll, and after her third, Beth was tipsy, bordering on drunk. She knew she was heading for inebriation because her nose was going numb. It was a sure sign she should stop. But she was having too much fun. She hadn't let her hair down like this in ages. Walter had recovered from his ordeal and was regaling her with stories about when he used to own the farm.

Many of them made her laugh, but a few were rather poignant, and when he talked about his wife, Beth could hear the pain in his voice and her heart went out to him.

'I still miss her,' he said, his eyes damp. 'Do you miss your husband?'

Beth shook her head. 'I'd just started divorce proceedings when he died. He was a waste of space – although I'd never tell the kids that. He spent most of his life, and most of his money, in the bookies. The irony was, he'd had a bit of luck on the horses the day he was killed. He'd watched the race in the pub over the road and was on his way to collect his winnings, when he stepped into the street without looking. His winnings paid for his funeral.'

Walter put a hand on hers. 'You must have had it tough, bringing up four kids on your own.'

'I coped.' It had been hard, but her children had never gone without.

Walter squeezed her hand. 'They're a credit to you.'

Yes, she thought, they were. Even Maisie, whom she had lain awake night after night worrying about, had settled down. Adam was a good man. Although Nikki's first husband had been useless and Beth had fretted that her eldest girl had married a wrong 'un, Nikki had eventually seen sense and had got shot of him. Beth thoroughly approved of Gio, her new partner. She approved of Otto, too.

'And Otto is a credit to **you**,' she told Walter. 'He's done incredibly well for himself.'

'Despite having me for a father,' Walter lamented.

'Don't say that. You did the best you could.'

'I lost the farm.'

'He's got it back. I wonder if we'll hear the sound of wedding bells soon?'

'I hope so. I think the world of Dulcie.' Walter paused to take a sip of his drink. He had moved on to Guinness, and it left a foam moustache on his upper lip.

Beth leant across the table and wiped it away.

Walter caught her hand mid-wipe and brought it to his lips. When he kissed her fingers, a thrill tingled right through her.

He said, 'Thank you for all your help. I couldn't have managed without you. I can't believe I'm saying this, but I've enjoyed your stay in the cottage and I'll miss you when you leave.'

Beth's eyes filled up. She would miss him too.

Who'd have thought it!

CHAPTER NINE

Beth raised her face to the sun and closed her eyes, feeling the welcome warmth on her skin. It was peaceful in Walter's garden, just the drone of insects and the occasional bleat from Flossie, who was missing her little goaty friends. Petra had taken them to the stables to have their hooves trimmed, leaving the sheep on her own for the morning. Flossie wasn't happy and was letting everyone know.

Walter was in the garden with Beth, reading his newspaper and huffing now and again when he came across an article he didn't like. Since the weather had become warmer, they'd taken to coming into the garden for an hour after breakfast if they didn't have anywhere to be.

Today was a quiet day. Beth had chores to do in the house, and later she would take Peg for a walk. She quite fancied going further afield and calling in on Maisie. She would drop her a text later and ask whether she would be in this afternoon.

A few more minutes, then she'd get a move on. It was a perfect day for drying washing and she had a mind to put fresh sheets on both their beds. Beth was quite content sitting here, though. She was quite content, full stop.

Without opening her eyes, she said, 'Do you realise it's exactly a month today since I moved in with you?' Not moved in, as such, because her living here was a temporary arrangement, but Walter would know what she meant.

'A month? It feels like longer.'

Beth's eyes flew open.

'In a good way,' he added hastily.

She closed them again. 'It does,' she agreed.

Yet at the same time, the month had flown by. Soon Walter's cast would be coming off and although he would continue to use crutches for a while, he would become increasingly more mobile and increasingly less dependent on her.

Beth suspected that he could manage most things well enough on his own now anyway, but she hadn't mentioned it and neither had he. Both of them were far too comfortable with their current arrangement to want it to change. Sharing Walter's house was preferable to living with Dulcie – although Beth never thought she'd hear herself say that.

She was about to begin her chores, when her phone rang. She had left it in the kitchen and hurried inside to answer it.

The number on the screen made her pause, and for one ridiculous second she was tempted to ignore it. However, it couldn't be ignored forever. They would call back and eventually she would have to answer.

'Hello?'

'Mrs Fairfax? It's Zander. I thought you'd like to know that all the repairs on the house in Hazelnut Road have been completed. I've just been out to check, and I'm happy to say that you can move in whenever you're ready.'

'Oh, great. Thanks. I'll, um, pop in for the keys.'

Although she had been expecting a phone call at some point, now that she had received it Beth wasn't sure how she felt. She should be delighted. But she wasn't. She felt flat. Sad, almost.

As she thought about the little terraced house, she could no longer imagine herself

living there. It wouldn't feel like home.
Walter's cottage felt like home. And
despite the new friends she had made and
the active social life she now had, she
feared she would be lonely living on her
own.

With a heavy heart she returned to the
garden to tell Walter the news.

'Beth doesn't mind taking me,' Walter said
to Otto for the third time that morning.

'I want to take you, Dad. I'd like to be
there when they remove the cast, so we
know how best to help you when Beth
moves out.'

'I don't need any help.' Walter knew he
was being surly and ungrateful, but he
couldn't help how he felt. He didn't want
Beth to leave. But if she had to (and he
knew that she did), he wasn't going to be

railroaded into moving into the farmhouse for a few days, or having anyone stay here. It was Beth, or no one.

And he was beginning to think that no one might be preferable to Beth, because since she had given him the news four days ago, they seemed to have reverted to their sniping, carping ways. It was as though the past month had been a dream. The way things were going at the moment, he might actually be glad to see the back of her.

So, maybe her moving out was better for everyone. But, despite trying to convince himself of that, he still didn't want her to go.

Beth, on the other hand, appeared eager. She had arranged a van and a couple of blokes to move her stuff and had spent the last three days cleaning both Walter's cottage and the house in the village. He hadn't realised his place was so dirty.

It had given him a pang to see her cases packed, ready for the move tomorrow. The house would feel empty without her.

'Dad, come on,' Otto urged. 'We're going to be late.'

Walter pressed his lips together grabbed his crutches and followed Otto outside.

As they got in the car Otto said, 'I hear Beth has been stocking your freezer for you.'

'Hmph.'

'That's kind of her, isn't it?'

'Stop being so patronising.'

Otto looked shocked. 'I'm not. I was simply making an observation.'

'You were speaking to me like I'm five years old.'

'I don't know what's got into you lately. Are you worried you won't cope on your own?'

'Grr.' Walter gritted his teeth.

'Dulcie and I will make sure you're okay.'

'I don't need anyone checking up on me. I'll be fine.'

'You're still going to need a bit of help. It'll be a while before you will be able to put much weight on that leg. Then there's the physio and the exercises you'll have to do.'

Walter took a deep breath. He knew Otto's comments were coming from a place of love. He knew Otto worried about him, and he knew he deserved all this fussing because his track record of taking care of himself in the past hadn't been great.

But without the farm to run and the associated money issues, things were different now. Otto didn't need to worry. Walter could take care of himself. And once the cast was off, he would soon be back to his pre-accident self. He would have his house all to himself again, and he wouldn't have to consider anyone else. He could put the kitchen cupboards back the way they were (Beth kept changing them), there wouldn't be any mysterious potions and lotions in the bathroom, and no having to watch Beth's smalls blowing on the line next to his. His house would be nice and peaceful again.

But was that really what he wanted?

'Bye, then.' Beth wondered whether she should give Walter a hug. Maybe not: he didn't come across as a hugger. She settled for a smile and a self-conscious wave instead.

'Good luck in your new home.'

'You'll have to come visit when I've settled in.'

'I will.'

Beth was fairly certain he wouldn't. 'Will I see you at Half Board?' Her gaze flickered to his leg, now free of its cast.

'Maybe.'

'If it's transport that you're worried about, I can fetch you and bring you back.'

'We'll see.'

'And if you need me to take you to your physio appointments, just ask. You've got my number.'

'Thanks.'

'Okay, then, I'll be off. Take care, Walter.'

'You, too.'

The exchange had been stilted and awkward, and by the time Beth had opened her car door, Walter had gone back inside the cottage.

'You're welcome,' she muttered. After everything she had done for him, Walter hadn't even thanked her. He'd waved her off without a second glance.

Irritated and feeling rather flat, Beth drove to her new house in the village. She had been looking forward to this day for such a long time, but now it seemed something of an anticlimax.

With a feeling of deja vu, Beth pulled into the kerb near the house on Hazelnut Road and cut the engine.

'Here we go again,' she said, seeing the van arrive in her rear-view mirror.

She had just unlocked the door and stepped inside, when she sensed someone behind her. Assuming it was one of the removal men, she glanced over her shoulder and was shocked to discover Dulcie and Maisie. And behind them were Otto and Adam.

'We've come to give you a hand, Mum,' Dulcie said.

Maisie added, 'You didn't think we'd let you move house on your own?'

It hadn't occurred to Beth to ask for their help, but it was very welcome nevertheless, and she was touched that her daughters were here.

'Nikki says she'll pop in to see you after school,' Dulcie said.

Beth felt the prick of tears and she swallowed hard. How could she have ever thought that her daughters wouldn't want her living near them?

'Where do you want this, love?' a gruff voice asked, and everyone hurriedly moved out of the way as two burly men manhandled her sofa through the front door.

'Just there, please.' Beth pointed to a spot in front of the fireplace, and when they set it down, she shoved one end until it was at the perfect angle.

After that there wasn't any time to think, as a succession of boxes, white goods and pieces of furniture were ferried into the house. Beth directed proceedings, darting upstairs and downstairs, then back again to ensure everything was placed where she wanted it.

In much less time than she had anticipated, the van had been unloaded and most of her things had been put away.

Adam was on his hands and knees connecting the telly, when Dulcie suggested a break.

'I'll put the kettle on,' Beth said and bustled into the kitchen, wondering which cupboard held the mugs.

She needn't have worried, because no one would be having a hot drink. Otto was opening a bottle of champagne, and the pop of a cork made her jump.

'Here's to your new home,' he said, pouring the sparkling liquid into tall flutes. He handed the first one to her.

Beth took it, her lip wobbling. 'I didn't expect this.'

'I know you didn't,' Dulcie laughed. 'You had hoped to fly in under the radar, and you would have done if the ceiling hadn't come down.'

Everyone looked up at it.

'You'd never know.' Adam said. 'They've done a good job.'

'They took their time,' Beth grumbled.

Otto said, 'I bet my dad is glad they did, otherwise you would have moved in sooner, and he would have ended up back with us.'

Beth said, 'I bet he's not. He couldn't wait to get rid of me this morning.'

'Don't you believe it! He's gutted.' That was from Dulcie.

'Only because he'll have to make his own cups of tea from now on.'

Dulcie was looking at her oddly. 'I thought you two were getting on better.'

Beth had thought so, too. She had been wrong. Now that her services were no longer required, the cease-fire was over.

It was gloves off once more.

Beth sat on the sofa in her new living room, a mug of cocoa on the table next to her, the TV remote in her hand as she flicked through the channels. She was tired, but she was also restless. This would be her first night in her new house, and she guessed it might take her a while to get used to the place. And to being on her own. It was strange how quickly she had become used to someone else's presence.

Or maybe not. After all, Maisie hadn't left home too long ago. But then again, when she had lived there, Maisie hadn't been in much. Always out gallivanting, that one. Gallivanting... Her own mum, the kids' grandmother, used to accuse her of doing the same thing. Beth had always had somewhere to go, and someone to go there with. Those were the days when she had been young, free and single. The only one of those things she could lay claim to now, was the single bit. Her youth had disappeared under the weight of being a wife and a mother, and the decades in between. She had been single after the kids' father had passed away, but it hadn't bothered her then because she had been too busy getting through the days.

It bothered her now, though. The month she had spent with Walter had made her realise that her loneliness hadn't gone away; it was still there, despite having three of her four children on her doorstep.

The house had been full when they had helped her unpack, but they couldn't stay forever. They had returned to their own lives, their own homes, and their own loves, leaving her alone and lonely once more.

Turning the telly off in irritation, she wondered what Walter was doing now. Revelling in having his house all to himself? Or wishing she had been there to warm up the casserole she had left him for his supper?

The first, probably.

And with that she finished her cocoa and took herself off to bed.

'How are you coping, Dad?'

'Fine.' Walter was glad that this was a phone call and Otto couldn't see him roll his eyes.

'Is there anything you need?'

'I could do with some milk and bread.'

'I'll drop them in on the way home from the restaurant this evening, if you're still up.'

'I'll be up.'

'Or I could pop in tomorrow?'

'Whatever suits you best, Otto.' Walter didn't mind either way; he would be pleased to see him regardless.

Amos and Lena had called in yesterday and they'd had a nice chat, but in the three days since Beth had left, time had dragged. It would be better when he was able to get out and about, he told himself. At the moment he couldn't walk far because he wasn't able to put much weight on his bad leg and he was still reliant on crutches, and neither could he drive yet. So he was stuck in the house.

Amos had kindly offered to have Peg for a couple of hours, so although Amos hadn't been taking her for an actual walk, she had been able to potter around the stables with Petra's dog Queenie. Walter felt quite envious. It came to something when his dog had more of a social life than he did.

Maybe he should go to Half Board tomorrow? Get out of the house for a bit. He could have a taxi there and back. Beth would probably be there, and the thought of seeing her made his heart leap. How was she getting on in her new house, he wondered. He had offhandedly asked Otto, who had told him that he'd helped her move in, along with Dulcie, Maisie and Adam, and they'd all had a glass of bubbly afterwards to toast her new home.

Walter felt quite put out that he hadn't been invited, despite knowing that he would only have been in the way and would have been as much use as a chocolate teapot.

Remembering her offer to take him to Half Board, he reached for his phone, but chickened out before he made the call. She had probably only offered out of a sense of obligation, considering she had taken him the other times he'd gone. He bet she didn't expect him to take her up on it.

His hand dropped to his side and he let out a despondent sigh. Having his house back wasn't living up to expectations. He had assumed he would enjoy the peace and quiet.

How wrong he had been.

The peace was like a heavy blanket, slowly suffocating him in loneliness, and the quiet was like a precursor to the grave. He was rattling around in the house, each room emptier than the last. It didn't help that he kept expecting Beth to walk through the door, or see her pottering in the kitchen, and he had lost count of the number of times he'd thought he'd heard her tread on the stairs, or smelt her perfume, only to find that his senses had deceived him.

A knock on the door made his heart surge with hope, and although he was pleased to see Amos, who had brought Peg back, a part of him had hoped it might have been Beth. A stupid part, because why would Beth want to visit **him?**

'Are you okay?' Amos was studying him.

'I'm fine.' Walter bent to ruffle Peg's ears. She licked him on the hand and dashed inside. A second later she was back, her tail down. She looked forlorn. 'I think she's missing Beth.'

Amos gave him a keen look. 'She's not the only one, I warrant.'

Walter let out a snort. 'As if.'

'Have it your way, but you were a happier bloke when she was around.'

'Never!'

Amos shooed him inside. 'Put the kettle on. The least you can do is make me a cuppa after I've minded your dog this morning.'

Walter scowled at his old friend but didn't argue.

'Have you heard from Eliza?' Amos asked, and Walter was glad to change the subject.

'I have. She's doing great! Five months pregnant now.' He sobered. 'I wish Emrys was here to see it. He would have been chuffed.' Walter's brother had emigrated to New Zealand thirty-odd years ago, and had died there a couple of years back. Eliza was his daughter. She had visited Picklewick at Christmas, searching for her father's roots, and had found love in the form of Jay, Beth's son.

It was strange to think of the ties that bound Walter and Beth together: Otto and Dulcie, Eliza and Jay... When Dulcie had won Lilac Tree Farm in the lottery, Walter could never have imagined how rich his life would become. He now had a whole new family, Beth included.

But he didn't actually think of Beth as family, though. He thought of her as... The word eluded him.

'It'll be Otto and Dulcie's turn next,' Amos was saying. 'There will be the patter of tiny feet at the farm.'

Walter chuckled. 'The only tiny feet Dulcie is interested in at the moment belong to the goats.'

'Pity. I think you could do with a grandchild to keep you occupied, and to keep you company.'

'I'm fine as I am.' He **would** like a grandchild, though.

'You can't fool me, Walter York; I've known you too long. It's not too late, you know.'

'Too late for what?'

'Love.'

 'You're talking out of your backside.'

Amos ignored him. 'Look at me and Lena. Who would have thought we'd ever get together. Yet here we are.'

'I don't think of Beth like that.'

Amos got to his feet. 'You do; you just can't admit it.'

Thankfully Stanley was fully clothed for the art class today, and neither was he posing. He was sitting at an easel, staring at the basket of fruit arrangement that was on a table in the middle of the room.

Beth thought the subject of today's composition was considerably more boring.

She hadn't been back to the art class since that first time with Walter, but boredom and loneliness had driven her out of the house. There was only so much cleaning and baking one could do, and her girls were all at work so she couldn't pop in to see them either. She had considered driving up Muddypuddle Lane to visit Walter, but she didn't know whether she would be welcome.

It was daft to miss him so much, but she couldn't help how she felt. The question she didn't have an answer to though, was did she miss him for himself, or did she miss looking after someone – anyone?

It surprised and dismayed her to realise that she felt lonelier in Picklewick than she had felt in Birmingham. How was that possible? There was an ache in her chest that she couldn't explain, a kind of longing, but she didn't know for what.

'Walter not with you today?' Stanley asked, his eyes lighting up when he saw her.

'Not today.'

'Did I put him off?'

'Pardon?'

He nodded at his crotch. 'Not everyone is as well endowed. Some men feel threatened or inadequate.'

Beth coloured, but she rallied quickly. 'Walter doesn't need to worry on that score,' she replied, with a suggestive wink.

Stanley's face fell. Clearly that wasn't the response he had expected. 'So, are you two an item?'

Beth simpered and smiled coyly. Let him make of that what he would. She had met men like Stanley before; the slightest encouragement and he'd be sniffing around her like a dog searching for leftovers in a bin. But if he thought she was unavailable, he'd look elsewhere for his entertainment.

Stanley nodded slowly, his expression solemn. 'I'm pleased for him. Walter deserves a second chance of happiness.'

Beth's eyes widened. Gosh, that was profound.

'Treat him right, Beth,' Stanley said. He brightened. 'But if you get fed up with his cranky farmer ways, you know where to find me.'

 'Right. Thanks.' What else could she say?

'You make a lovely couple, by the way,' he added.

'You do,' Melanie said, making Beth jump. She hadn't realised the art teacher was so close. 'I wish I had a fella who looked at me the way Walter looks at you. That's love for you – makes me go all gooey-eyed. It's a shame he's not here today; I loved his caricature of Stanley.' Stanley scowled as Melanie continued, 'I'd like to see what he could do with a basket of fruit, but I suspect still life isn't his speciality.'

Beth had stopped listening. She was stuck on the word **love**. It couldn't be true. The woman was talking out of her backside. Walter didn't love her. He didn't particularly like her. But for Stanley and Melanie to think the same thing…

Could there be some truth to it? Did Walter have feelings for her?

The thought made her knees go weak and she had to sit down. Shuffling towards the nearest unoccupied easel, she plopped onto the chair. Her pulse was racing and there was an odd sensation in her tummy. Her heart felt full and the ache in her chest was one she hadn't experienced in decades. So it wasn't surprising that it took her a while to understand what it signified.

Beth was in love.

The realisation caught her unawares, and she froze.

Suddenly everything made sense – the loneliness, the restlessness, the longing for something she couldn't name...

 And, Beth being Beth, there was only one thing for it – she had to speak to Walter.

Leaping to her feet, she ran out of the room, ignoring the startled looks of her fellow artists, and raced home to fetch her car.

Cursing at the slow-moving traffic in the high street, she put her foot down when she left the village and was soon zooming up Muddypuddle Lane, before coming to an abrupt halt as she slammed on the brakes outside Walter's cottage.

It was then that her courage failed her, and she began to question her impulsive flight. What kind of madness had overtaken her? All it had taken were a few misguided and ill-informed comments, and she was daft enough to believe that Walter might have feelings for her. She was behaving like a schoolgirl with a crush. And she had been about to make a total and utter fool of herself. Thank goodness she had come to her senses in time.

Taking a moment to catch her breath and tame her too-fast heart, she closed her eyes, willing herself to calm down. She would go home, have a nice cup of tea, watch some drivel on the telly, and try to forget that she loved Walter.

Knuckles rapped on the driver's window and Beth's eyes flew open as she uttered a shriek.

Walter was peering in at her. 'Beth?' He made a wind-the-window-down motion.

She wound it down.

'Did you forget something?' he asked.

'No, I...' She trailed off. 'I shouldn't have come. Sorry.'

'Would you like a cup of tea, since you're here? I've got your favourites, pink wafers. And Peg would like to see you. She's missed you.'

'At least someone has,' Beth muttered.

'**I've** missed you too.'

'You have?'

Walter nodded. 'The house is empty without you.'

Beth stared at him, trying not to read too much into it.

'So is my heart,' he added.

Beth blinked. 'Excuse me?'

He froze, his expression closed. 'Never mind. I shouldn't have said anything.' He turned away and she heard him mumble, 'Stupid, so stupid.'

'Walter!' Her voice was sharp, but she couldn't leave it like that. She couldn't leave **him.** She had to know if he meant what he'd said.

He stopped, his back to her.

'Do you love me?' she called, amazed and frightened at her boldness, dreading his reply. If he said no, if she'd got it wrong, she didn't know how she would be able to face him again. She would die of embarrassment. Or possibly a broken heart. Either way, the result wouldn't be pretty.

She saw his shoulders stiffen, read the tension in his back, and feared the answer.

'Yes.' Then a low, almost furious, 'God help me.' She guessed he didn't want to love her but he couldn't help himself. She understood that, because she felt the same way.

'And I love **you**, Walter.'

He didn't turn around, not for a long time, and the silence stretched between them.

Peg broke it. The dog came charging out of the house, thundered past Walter and threw herself at the car door, whimpering ecstatically.

In slow motion, Beth watched Walter topple as the dog unbalanced him.

Beth was out of the car in a second, pushing Peg away as she knelt beside him. 'Are you hurt?' she cried, scouring his face for signs of pain.

'Only my pride. Damned dog. I swear she likes you better than me.' He was on his side, gazing up at her, his expression as grumpy as when she'd first met him.

It made her laugh. 'Thank goodness. For a minute, I thought I'd have to move back in.'

'Would that be so bad?'

'No...'

'I love you, Beth.' He pushed himself into a sitting position, as Beth fended off Peg's enthusiastic licks. 'Peg's a good judge of character,' Walter said. 'She's been pining after you.' He looked deep into her eyes. 'So have I. Can I kiss you?'

'I think you should. But can I get up first? There's a lump of gravel poking me in the bum.'

It took Beth two attempts to get to her feet, and Walter three. She had to help him up.

'Are you sure you're okay?' she asked.

'I am now. How about that kiss?'

'Go on then. And afterwards you can make me the cup of tea you promised, and I'll have two pink wafers, please.'

'You're wish is my command. **I'm** going to look after **you** for a change.'

Beth's hand slipped into his. 'How about we look after each other?' she suggested. 'That's what married folk do.'

'Beth Fairfax, are you proposing to me?'

'Not on your nelly! If there's any proposing to be done, I expect **you** to do it. Anyway, I would probably say no – after all, we can't stand the sight of each other, can we?'

'Nope, that's why I'm going to close my eyes when I kiss you. Now, stop talking woman, and pucker up.'

'What's going on, Mum?' Dulcie's gaze roamed over Beth's face, then Walter's. 'Why have you called a **family meeting**?' She did air quotes with her fingers.

 It was Sunday morning, and Beth was well aware that everyone in her family were busy people. But they could spare her half an hour. 'I'll tell you when Nikki gets here,' she said.

'I see you picked Walter up on the way,' Maisie observed. 'It's nice that the two of you get on.'

Beth bit back a smile and ignored the hip bump Walter gave her. 'Get the kettle on,' was all she said.

'It's on.' Dulcie rinsed out the teapot. She was adding a couple of fresh teabags when Sammy and his dog burst in through the door, Nikki and Gio following.

'Are we having a party?' he cried.

'No party, Sammy.' Beth gathered him to her, inhaling his little boy smell and swearing that he'd grown since the last time she'd seen him.

'Can we have one?' he persisted.

'Not right now, your nanna has got something to tell us.' Nikki was looking concerned.

'Make the tea and bring it into the living room,' Beth instructed, ushering Walter ahead of her.

'You're enjoying this,' he murmured out of the corner of his mouth. 'They're probably taking bets on what it's about. Do you think any of them have guessed?

'I expect so. But it's nice to make it official. They can gossip amongst themselves after we've left.'

Dulcie appeared with a tray and began to pour. Once or twice, she opened her mouth to speak, but Beth quelled her with a look.

When everyone had a drink in their hands, Beth cleared her throat. 'We've got an announcement,' she said, then paused for dramatic effect. 'I've moved in with Walter. Permanently. We're a couple.'

'A couple of what?'

'Don't be dense, Maisie – a **couple**, couple.'

Maisie's mouth fell open. 'Oh, **that** kind of couple. Bloody hell, Otto, you were right. I thought you were pulling our legs.'

Walter turned to his son. 'You guessed?'

'I **knew**. I've known from the minute you two met. It was just a question of time, wasn't it, Dulcie?'

Beth stared at her middle daughter and everything clicked into place. 'You set us up!' she accused. 'You knew I'd agree to help Walter out, if only to get rid of him. Dulcie Fairfax, you conniving, sneaky—'

A cork popped. Otto was opening a bottle of champagne for the second time in a week. 'I think this calls for a celebration.'

'Hang fire a minute,' Walter said. 'There's more.'

Beth took up the baton. 'As I'm living with Walter now, I'm not going to need my house in the village.'

A chorus of groans erupted, and Dulcie cried, 'Don't tell me we have to help you move again.'

'Not necessarily,' Beth said. She glanced at the faces of her family, settling on Maisie. 'My tenancy agreement was for six months initially, so there's no point in moving all my furniture again if I've got to pay the rent on it for half a year.'

Dulcie said, 'Can't you get out of it? It seems silly to pay rent if you're not living there.'

'Unfortunately, I can't,' Beth replied. 'Anyway, I'm happy to continue paying it, especially if someone else is living there.'

'Who?' Nikki demanded.

Beth focused on Maisie again. 'Maisie, Adam, how much longer until the old farmhouse is ready to live in?'

Maisie shrugged. 'I dunno... Five, six months.' Beth grinned as realisation dawned on her youngest child's face. 'Are you saying that me and Adam can live in your house in the village?'

'I am. I've spoken to the estate agent and it will take a bit of rejigging of the contract, but it can be done. If you want to live there rather than in that cramped and dingy caravan whilst you do your house up, you can.'

Maisie's eyes filled with tears and she leapt up to give Beth a hug. 'That's so kind of you, Mum,' she sobbed. 'We can't thank you enough.'

Beth added, 'I'll take the bits and pieces I want and move them into Walter's cottage, but you can have the rest. They'll do you for the time being, and what you don't want, you can get rid of.'

'Thanks, Mum,' Maisie said, sniffling. 'We'll be able to live in comfort until we can move into our forever home.' Then she let out a gasp. **'That's it!** That's the perfect name for our new place – The Forever Home. We've been trying to think what to call it.'

Everyone began talking at once, and with a meaningful glance at Beth, Walter and he left them to it.

'They seemed happy for us,' Beth said when they were outside. 'I can't believe Dulcie and Otto were so sly.'

Walter took her in his arms. 'I'm so glad they were. We might have got there on our own, but it could have taken a while. Who knows how much time we would have wasted bickering at each other?' He kissed her on the cheek. 'Come on, let's go home to **your** forever home.'

As she drove the short distance to Walter's little cottage, Beth realised that Walter was right; it was her home now. And by coming to Picklewick, both she and Walter had a second chance at love, and this time she knew it would last forever. Even if they did bicker now and again...

There are loads more large print books in the Muddypuddle Lane series. Available at all good book stores, or ask your local library.

About Etti

Etti Summers is the author of wonderfully romantic fiction with happy ever afters guaranteed.

She is also a wife, a mum, a pink gin enthusiast, a veggie grower and a keen reader.